ELON MUSK

(Almost)

SAVES *the* WORLD

By Lucien Young

The Downing Street Guide to Party Etiquette

The Secret Diary of Boris Johnson Aged 13¼

#Sonnets

The Secret Diary of Jeremy Corbyn

Trump's Christmas Carol

Alice in Brexitland

LUCIEN YOUNG

ELON MUSK
(Almost)
SAVES *the* WORLD

WILDFIRE

First published in 2022 by
WILDFIRE
an imprint of HEADLINE PUBLISHING GROUP

1

Cataloguing in Publication Data is available from the British Library

Hardback ISBN 978 1 0354 0227 4

Illustrations by Luke Brookes
Cover by Marcus Scudamore

Designed and set by EM&EN
Printed and bound in Great Britain by Clays Ltd, Elcograf S.p.A.

Headline's policy is to use papers that are natural, renewable and recyclable
products and made from wood grown in well-managed forests and other
controlled sources. The logging and manufacturing processes are expected
to conform to the environmental regulations of the country of origin.

HEADLINE PUBLISHING GROUP
An Hachette UK Company
Carmelite House
50 Victoria Embankment
London EC4Y 0DZ

www.headline.co.uk
www.hachette.co.uk

Disclaimer

The following is a lighthearted spoof of pulp sci-fi novels. If real-world figures are depicted as reckless fools or cackling supervillains, this is merely the author bowing to genre convention.

CONTENTS

INTRODUCTION

Everyone's favourite businessman makes his pulse-pounding debut in this dazzling work of scientifiction. It's the epic adventure a million rabid fanboys have been waiting for.

GASP at the world's richest man as he traverses the stars in his electric space vehicle, *Icarus 1*!

MARVEL at the lofty promises made by this 51-year-old whiz-kid!

PREPARE for action, romance and endless publicity stunts!

Elon is the suavest, most scintillating hero in all of fantasy. And rest assured: his glamorous companions will be along for the ride! These include

AARS the robot butler, GURK the half-dog body-guard, and PRINCESS GRIMES, interstellar siren.

He'll also face the deadliest adversaries the galaxy has to offer, from the fiendish VORNAX to a mysterious human foe (JEFF BEZOS). But fear not, dear reader: anyone who stands in his way will either be vaporised or called a 'pedo guy' on Twitter.

Elon Musk (Almost) Saves the World is the first book in a proposed series of two hundred. Why not buy copies for yourself and several other Musketeers? Together we can prove, once and for all, that billionaires deserve their wealth and should be in charge of every aspect of our lives!

PROLOGUE

It was a typical day in New York City. Your classic, run-of-the-mill, dime-a-dozen sort of day. Certainly not a day on which you might expect an alien spaceship to appear and change the course of human history. So, when that did happen, people were understandably upset.

Around lunchtime, a booming sound was heard across the Eastern Seaboard. A colossal vessel, ovoid and obsidian, descended from the atmosphere and came to rest above Central Park. It was five miles in height and cast a shadow from Times Square to the Statue of Liberty. All over the city, New Yorkers gawped and pointed at this apparition.

'Ay, whoa, I'm looking at a frickin' UFO over here!' exclaimed a hot-dog vendor, the sausage dropping from his tongs.

'Oof, *marone*!' cried the mobster, spraying cannoli over the guy he just whacked.

'Sell! Sell sell sell!' clamoured the Wall Street traders, worried about what first contact would do to the NASDAQ.

Naturally, the most common reaction was to whip out one's phone and start streaming.

Within minutes, images of the looming, egg-shaped craft were beamed around the world, occasioning cries of *'Incrível'* in Rio de Janeiro and *'Sugoi'* in Yokohama. The general emotion was fear. Everyone had seen the movies: *Independence Day*, *War of the Worlds*, *Mars Attacks!* When an alien dreadnought hove into view, it was seldom good news for Earth's population.

Anticipating enslavement, or even disintegration, millions retreated to bomb shelters, gathered pitchforks and baseball bats, or prayed to their various gods. But one corner of the internet was free of any such terror. This oasis of calm could be found on Reddit, specifically r/elonmusk. A million Redditors, tapping away in their parents' garage or on the toilet, greeted the news of extraterrestrial life with complete equanimity.

'Don't worry, guys,' read one representative post: 'Elon will save us.'

1

THE WIZARD OF MARS

Olympus Mons: the tallest mountain in the solar system, two-and-a-half times the height of Everest. This had been the most impressive fact about the shield volcano until five years ago, when Earth's greatest genius, Elon Musk, decided to make his home there. Xanadu Base sat in the central caldera, gleaming like a diamond against the rust-red landscape. Musk had designed it as an outpost, a seed that would grow into mankind's first off-world colony. It was never his intention to take up residence there. However, tired of baseless criticism and shareholder lawsuits, he became determined to slip the surly bonds of Earth. In 2023, Elon had upped sticks and moved to Mars. Amid the silence of the red planet, he was free to think his massive thoughts in peace, unencumbered by lesser minds.

Now the year was 2028, and Musk had few regrets concerning his Martian sojourn. Indeed, that period had seen him at his most creatively fecund. Brilliant new ideas burst from his head: self-zipping trousers, bacon-flavoured beer, jet-packs that could be used by toddlers. He knew with absolute certainty that these inventions would revolutionise human existence and usher mankind towards a brighter future. And if they made him even more rich and famous, where was the harm in that? After all, he was the man who invented the electric car. Well, not technically, but he did have the idea to charge $100,000 for them.

Very occasionally he found himself missing some aspect of Earth life: an evening spent in fellowship, say, or the embrace of a good woman. But these complaints paled in comparison to Elon's glorious purpose. He was fated to achieve the impossible and render *homo sapiens* an inter-planetary species. Though he was too humble to admit it, Elon well understood that he was closer to a god than a man. While surveying his domain through one of Xanadu's vast Duraglass windows, he would often reflect on his similarity to Dr Manhattan from Alan Moore's *Watchmen*. It was the sort of nerdy reference that made his heart sing. 'Hell yeah,' he would murmur to himself. 'That's freaking epic.'

Elon may have been the only human on Mars, but he was never truly alone. When making the voyage from Earth, he had brought his two closest comrades, Gurk and Aars. Gurk was half human, half canine, a genetic hybrid created by mistake in one of Musk's laboratories. The scientists had wanted to destroy this hideous chimera, but Elon took pity, raising him from a baby-puppy to a man-dog. Nowadays Gurk was eight feet tall, possessed of superhuman – and supercanine – strength. As such, he had been designated Elon's personal bodyguard and Head of Security. Gurk fulfilled these roles admirably, despite the constant pain of his unnatural existence, and his tendency to sniff butts.

Aars was Elon's butler, his name an acronym for Augmented Autonomous Robot Servant. As a lonely ten-year-old in Pretoria, Musk had built the polished-silver android to be his friend and constantly assure him of his genius. Effete, nervy and obsequious, Aars was the polar opposite of gruff, laconic Gurk.

Though Elon couldn't be said to love anyone – he was beyond such trivial attachments – he was nonetheless fond of his inhuman companions. Gurk and Aars were essential to his research, and thus the future of mankind. Also, with Aars doing the cooking and cleaning, Elon had more time for Twitter. He spent, conservatively speaking, 80 per cent of his life on the notorious microblogging platform. Solving climate change and colonising planets was all well and good, but what was the point if he didn't talk about it constantly? Plus, he needed to share dank memes and clap back at his haters.

On 1 August, at 2 p.m. Martian Standard Time, Elon Musk entered his Tweeting Chamber. The spherical room was specially designed to maximise his posting abilities, allowing him to produce takes of unprecedented heat. He sank into his ergonomic chair, cracked his knuckles, and settled in for his customary five hours of name-searching*. Perchance some ten-follower account had cast aspersions on his business practices, or described his stint hosting SNL as 'brutally unfunny'. If so, that vile troll was about to face the collective fury of Elon's 100 million Stans. What he saw upon logging on banished such thoughts in an instant.

The first thing he noticed was the trending topics:

> #AlienInvasion
> #EndOfTheWorld
> #PrepareToBeProbed

Then there were the stunning images and videos that filled his feed. They showed a gargantuan ship, black and gleaming, which hung over New

---

* Twitter allows public figures to search their own names and see what millions of people are saying about them. Which is obviously great for their sanity.

York like the sword of Damocles. Naturally, some Twitter users were sceptical, accusing the mainstream media of confecting the UFO to promote woke vaccines and drag-queen abortions. But most on the platform accepted this alarming new reality. Aliens were now a thing, and we each had to respond in our own way. Some called for unconditional surrender. Others advocated a pre-emptive nuclear strike. Others still tweeted out invitations to hastily convened orgies.

His mind racing even faster than usual, Elon Musk checked his mentions. Notification after notification sprang up, too quickly to count. The panicked masses were tweeting at him, their voices combined in one huge chorus. 'Mr Musk,' begged @ElonFan420, 'return to Earth and protect mankind!' @TeslaJunkie69 concurred: 'Help us, Elon, you're our only hope!'

The great man allowed himself a smirk: '*Star Wars: Episode IV.* Nice.'

But it wasn't just the reference that stirred his heart. Reading these tweets, Elon Musk realised that he had missed something during his stay on

Mars. It wasn't conversation or physical intimacy, and it certainly wasn't making eye contact. No – Elon missed being needed. He missed being a hero.

Moments later, Elon Musk emerged from the Tweeting Chamber and greeted his inhuman servants with a wide grin.

'Aars, prepare my ship,' he exclaimed. 'I have a planet to save!'

2

HUMANITY'S HERO

Icarus 1, an electric rocket-ship of Elon's own design, blazed through the icy void of space. No craft devised by mortal mind could rival its velocity. Other ships struggled to make the journey from Mars to Earth in seven months. The *Icarus* would reach its destination within the runtime of *Spider-Man: No Way Home.*

In a transparent cockpit at the vehicle's nose sat Elon, resplendent in a scarlet-and-gold flight suit, whose fabric barely contained his ripped muscles and bulging crotch. Here, flying at 45 million miles per hour, he was in his element. Nobody disputed his claim to be Earth's greatest pilot. The only thing he knew better than a spaceship's controls was the female anatomy. But for all the pleasure that space-flight afforded him, Elon's mind was on graver things. He turned his handsome head, with its shock of natural hair. 'Aars, tweet the following from my account: *Don't worry, everyone, I'm monitoring the situation closely. It will be resolved soon.*'

Gurk looked quizzical, his tongue lolling out. 'But sir, how can you promise that? We don't know a damn thing about these aliens.'

Aars's metallic voice hissed with outrage: 'Silence, you demi-mutt! Master Elon is the smartest human in existence. He knows everything about everything.'

Elon grinned at the passionate android. 'I appreciate that, Aars. I know it came from the heart and not my programming.'

He turned his attention to the dog-man. 'And don't worry, Gurk. If there's one thing Elon Musk would never do, it's make wild promises that he has no means of fulfilling.'

Chastened, Gurk glanced at his monitor.

'Coming up on Earth in T-minus fifteen minutes. Ruff ruff! Bow wow!'

T

Joseph Robinette Biden Jr had the twin distinctions of being President of the United States and the world's oldest man. To cope with the demands of his job, he had been augmented with the latest Musk biotech: skin-tightening nanobots, artificial hair, synaptic boosters. While these devices did much to invigorate him, he was currently feeling the full weight of his years.

Within the Oval Office were gathered Biden's top aides, the Joint Chiefs of Staff and the world's leading experts on astrophysics, linguistics and xenology. Their goal was to determine a response to the arrival of an alien spacecraft over Central Park. Unfortunately, Old Joe hadn't the first idea what these Poindexters were going on about. It was a good thing he wore his aviator shades – if he happened to fall asleep, no one would be any the wiser.

One of the experts was midway through a treatise: 'These beings possess technological capabilities far in advance of our own, perhaps even faster-than-light travel. As such, any attempt at communication must be premised on the assumption –'

Biden raised a wrinkled hand.

'Now hold on just a moment, you . . . you . . . dog-faced pony soldier,' he said, presidentially. 'You're spraying around these words like . . . like a dictionary with diarrhoea. Back in the day, Scranton, man, you should have seen us. Me, Randy, Cornpop, Toadstool – we didn't need these ten-dollar words. For a nickel, you could get nouns, adjectives, prepositions. And you still had change to buy your sweetheart a root beer. Come on, man!'

In the silence that followed, each expert shifted uncomfortably in his or her seat. Peterson, the president's young aide, spoke up. 'Sir, that's very well put. To reiterate, we cannot allow ourselves to become bogged down with jargon. We must come to a decision and express it clearly and in action-able language.'

The experts weren't sure that this was what Biden meant, but opted to press on. Judith Rosenbaum, professor of international relations at Stanford, and the holder of five PhDs, cleared her throat.

'Mr President, I advise we proceed with a high degree of caution. We don't know what these aliens want, or whether they should be considered friend or foe. It's vital we open up lines of communication. But whoever we choose to make first contact will have to be someone of wisdom, patience, diplomatic skill and emotional maturity.'

Biden slumped in his big leather chair. He was growing tired of these eggheads and nap-time was fast approaching. Just then, a sonic boom rocked the building.

'Oh boy!' cried Biden, rushing to the window like a child on Christmas morning. From there he watched as *Icarus 1* came to land in the Rose Garden, incinerating most of the roses. Biden beamed, not sparing a thought for his flora.

'He came! He really came, no foolin'!'

T

Moments later, Elon strode into the Oval Office, Gurk and Aars in tow. Unfazed by the grandeur of his surroundings, he spoke in a magisterial tone. 'We've had a long trip. My companions require sustenance. Plug Aars in and give Gurk a meal: half haute cuisine, half dog food.'

'Whatever you say, Mr Musk!' exclaimed Biden. 'I'm just so thrilled you made it. Billionaire space-hero Elon Musk in my little office, wowee!'

The cosmic explorer marched over to the Resolute Desk and Biden happily relinquished his seat. 'Listen, Mac,' he said, 'we're in a pickle here. No, I'm serious, no joke. I don't know what the hell I'm doing. We've got li'l . . . little green men, flying around in . . . in the thing . . . I mean, these guys are like something outta . . . *Trek Wars*. So here's the deal: we need Elon, period.'

Peterson the aide looked nervous.

'Yes, sir, I'm sure Mr Musk's input will be very valuable. When combined with that of our other experts . . .'

'Horse apples!' cried Biden, suddenly furious.

'These bookworms have been gabbing for fifteen whole minutes and all I've heard is malarkey.'

The superannuated leader of the free world placed a hand on Musk's shoulder. 'Elon, you're the guy I trust to deal with these moon-men. You'll have all the resources of the United States behind you. So what do you say, son? Will you help Old Joe out?'

Peterson stepped forward, his face anguished. 'Again, sir, I highly recommend we coordinate with the International Space Agency instead of some private contractor. They can draw upon knowledge from all across the globe and –'

Elon snorted with derision. 'The ISA? Those virgins couldn't make contact with a boob, let alone an alien race. And how many qualified astrophysicists have you seen on Forbes list of billionaires?'

'He's right,' snapped Biden. 'Elon is the world's richest man, which means he's the smartest. Why would I listen to anyone but him?'

The experts raised a chorus of expert objections. Ignoring them, Elon leapt to his feet. 'Very well, Mr President. I, Elon Reeve Musk, Captain of the *Icarus*, Ruler of Mars, Traverser of the Untraversable, shall heed your call. I shall enter the alien mother ship, make first contact, and gauge their intentions. But all of this will be done my way. And I'll need a hundred billion dollars – I'm not about to save the world for free.'

'Hooray!' Biden rejoiced. 'I knew I could count on you!'

With that, Elon, Gurk and Aars strode purposefully out of the West Wing and back into *Icarus 1*. The mighty rockets flared, shattering every window in the building and scorching its white walls black. Biden grinned as the ship sped off at face-melting velocity.

'Elon Musk. What a man, man!'

T

Once most of the debris had been cleared, the presidential braintrust turned to public relations. How could they calm the country in the face of extraterrestrial incursion? Biden was adamant that he should address the American people directly, without notes or a prepared speech.

'I know how to give folks the skinny, Mac. I'll get on FaceTweet, Tic Tacs, let 'em know what's what. Cos these ain't the aliens you remember. ET. Mork from Ork. Those were good guys, sweet guys. The new ones they got nowadays, they make Roswell look like . . . summer camp. We're talking, take that probe, put it God knows where. Your butt. Man, I'm sorry, I shouldn't have said that. But seriously, no joke, I'm being serious. Don't let anyone up there 'cept a qualified physician. ALF, that's another one . . .'

Peterson winced. 'Perhaps we should stick to the teleprompter . . .'

3

INTO THE MOTHER SHIP

'I have a bad feeling about this,' Aars intoned. *Icarus 1* was gliding over New York City, towards the ebon mass that now dominated its skyline.

'Come come, Aars,' said Elon, 'I didn't program you to be a coward.'

'I don't like this either,' Gurk growled. 'How am I meant to ensure your safety once we board?'

'My safety is ensured by two things,' the billionaire replied. 'One is my silver tongue.'

'And the other?'

'This.'

Elon brandished his trusty electric raygun, capable of discharging 300,000 volts, then twirled it on his finger in a casual but impressive way. He brought the *Icarus* within a hundred metres of the alien ship and let it hover. The cyclopean vessel thrummed with malevolence.

'Sir, I suggest you begin your transmission,' Aars quivered.

Elon flicked a switch and spoke in his commanding baritone.

'This is Captain Elon Musk of the *Icarus*, requesting permission to board. We come in peace and I am unarmed.'

He winked at Gurk, tucking the raygun into his space suit. For what felt an eternity, there came no reply from the alien ship. Static hissed in the cockpit speakers.

'Oh well,' said Aars, 'it seems they aren't taking visitors. Perhaps we should give up and go back to Mars.'

Then, with no accompanying transmission, part of the jet-black hull opened to reveal a hangar.

'You see, Aars?' Elon chuckled. 'I always get what I want.'

T

Icarus 1 landed gracefully in the hangar, whose cavernous dimensions were dimly illuminated by a sinister green glow. A ramp lowered and Elon emerged, flanked by his buddies, the dog-man and the robot. Aars carried a pair of laser pistols, while Gurk wielded his trusty sonic hammer. Suddenly, a host of creatures materialised from the stygian dark. These aliens were humanoid in height and proportion, but there the resemblance ended. They were hairless, with huge, squid-like eyes and clawed, tridactyl hands. Most appalling to the human gaze were their mouths, or rather the mass of twitching feelers where mouths should be. The monsters spoke among themselves, each tentacled maw emitting a horrid squelching noise. This cacophony could hardly be considered language, and yet it seemed animated by fiendish intelligence.

'Did someone order calamari?' quipped Elon. Despite their overwhelming terror, Gurk and Aars laughed: he was very clever and very funny.

One of the space-things stepped forward. Unlike its fellows, who wore grey uniform, it was dressed in intricately patterned robes. In its three-fingered hand was an orb of pure white light. To Elon's surprise, the creature began to speak in perfect English, its tone rich and mellow.

'Greetings, E-lon, son of Errol. We are honoured by your presence. We have learned much about you from what Earthmen call "the internet".'

'All good, I hope?'

The alien paused, then moved on.

'I am an ambassador of the Vornax. We come to your planet as friends and benefactors. As you have been chosen to represent your species, I am instructed to bring you before our leader.'

'Take me to your leader,' mugged Elon.

The Vornax ambassador twitched its face-tentacles in confusion.

'I just said that I would.'

'Yeah, I know,' Elon replied, 'but I wanted to say the line.'

The ambassador bowed deeply and gestured towards an ornate entrance.

'This way, my lord.'

As Elon and his companions moved deeper into

the Vornax ship, he patted Aars on the shoulder. 'See? We're making friends already.'

Elon was chuffed with how cool he was being. Perhaps, when they inevitably made a film about this, he would be played by Chris Pratt.

T

The aliens escorted the trio down a long corridor, which eventually opened into a magnificent throne room. Every surface glittered with artefacts of a civilisation utterly foreign to humanity. There were courtiers with silver cloaks, as well as a row of guards bearing pikes. In the centre of it all sat a figure clad in gold, its facial tentacles far longer than the others. Though Elon knew nothing of Vornax hierarchies, it seemed clear this guy was in charge.

The ambassador climbed the steps to the throne, then turned back to the Earthlings.

'Kneel before King Klathu!'

Knowing their master would not take this well, Gurk and Aars cast beseeching looks in his direction. Elon gritted his teeth.

'Yeah, sorry, pal, that ain't happening.'

At this insolence, the Vornax gave a collective cry of outrage. The king's guards lowered their pikes and advanced, menacingly. Then Klathu made a single, authoritative squelch. In an instant, the crowd fell silent and the guards withdrew. The ambassador bowed, proffering his orb to Klathu, who took it in a bejewelled claw. He proceeded to address Elon in a voice almost identical to that of Laurence Fishburne.

'Very well – we need not stand on ceremony. I am king of all my species. I presume you are king of yours.'

'That's right,' said Elon. 'Hey, how come you speak English?'

'I am speaking Vornaxian,' the king replied. 'However, this device alters our brainwaves, allowing us to understand any language.'

Feeling a tad insecure, Elon began to bluster.

'Yeah, I guess that's kind of impressive. I mean, I've definitely invented cooler stuff, but it's a fun trifle.'

Aars cleared his throat (or rather, his speech circuits made the sound of throat-clearing).

'Master, perhaps you should state the reason for our visit.'

'Right, yes. King Klathu, I stand before you as emissary of the human race. On this planet's behalf, I request that you share your intentions in coming here.'

After a pause, the king pressed a button on the armrest of his throne. Blue holograms appeared, whirling around Elon in a cosmic ballet of stars and planets. It was a map, he realised, one of unimaginable scale.

'We Vornax come from the Andromeda galaxy,' Klathu narrated. 'Our home-world, Vornax Prime, was once a paradise. Great Bontos roamed the plains and Ithyllium trees cleansed the air. Then came the Cataclysm. It was a doom we brought upon ourselves, through the ceaseless engine of industry. While Vornax science let us explore the stars, it ruined our home. We survived ecological collapse, but what was lost could never be regained.'

It having been several minutes since he heard his own name, Elon yawned. Fortunately, the aliens did not recognise the gesture as disrespectful.

King Klathu continued: 'Decades ago, our astronomers detected intelligent life on a little blue planet orbiting Sol. That intelligent life was you.'

'You mean me specifically?'

'Humanity in general.'

'Oh. Okay.'

'There was much to admire about your civilisation. Curiosity. Creativity. Beauty. But there was also greed, belligerence, contempt for nature. Like us, you were sowing the seeds of your destruction. Upon ascending the throne, I decided we would voyage to Earth and give humanity what we never had.'

'Which is?'

'A chance to avert disaster. That is why the Vornax are here. To grant humans the tools and knowledge you need to ward off climate change, cure all diseases, and assume your place among the stars.'

Gurk turned to Musk, relief upon his doggy

visage. 'Well, I'll be damned,' he said. 'Turns out these guys are super nice.'

'Yes,' affirmed Aars, 'they just want to help us. What good fortune!'

Elon, however, was fuming. His skin blushed crimson and a vein bulged on his temple. Noticing this, Gurk and Aars attempted to calm him down.

'Sir, what's wrong?' whispered Gurk. 'Tell me and we can sort it out.'

'Please, master, don't do anything rash,' added Aars.

But Musk was unmoved by their entreaties. Fixing a contemptuous eye on the Vornax king, he began to shout: 'Screw you, Klathu! You bloody octopuses have some nerve, coming here and acting like your technology is so advanced. Like you're smarter than me!'

The king's feelers writhed wetly, a sign of confusion among his race. 'I mean, our technology is more advanced. And our cerebral capacity is fifty per cent greater than yours. But that doesn't mean we regard you as lesser –'

'Right, that's it!' Elon ejaculated. 'I hereby

command you to piss off. Crawl back to your shithole planet or I'll blow this ship out of the sky.'

Having glanced at his advisers in bafflement, Klathu turned to Elon.

'Perhaps my translation orb is malfunctioning. I'm saying we want to help you, with no strings attached.'

'And I'm saying, on behalf of Earth, we don't need your poxy help. So vamoose, you squid-faced prick, or else!'

One of the silver-cloaked Vornax stepped forward. With a rapid series of mouth-squelches, it laid a claw on Elon's shoulder. Acting on instinct, Musk whipped out his electric raygun and plugged the creature with 300,000 volts. It staggered back, stricken, a burning hole in its torso. With a moist exhalation, the alien fell down dead.

King Klathu screamed, dropping his orb and bounding down the steps. As he cradled his smouldering comrade, the ambassador picked up the orb and addressed Elon.

'Why did you do that? He was saying you shouldn't worry, that we could work all this out.'

Elon shrugged. 'Yeah, well, he shouldn't have snuck up. It was him or me, bro.'

Klathu let out a terrible, barbaric shriek, a clawed finger pointed accusingly.

'Why's he so butthurt?' asked Musk. 'All I did was kill one of his guards.'

The throng of Vornax made dark and ominous noises. Their ambassador spoke once more. 'That was Prince Zanzar, His Highness's only son.'

This revelation gave Elon pause. 'Oh. Well. Shit.'

He called over to Klathu: 'My condolences, Your Majesty. It was an unfortunate accident. Lots of people to blame.'

Vornax encircled our heroes: courtiers and guards with murder in their eyes. In their hands glinted strange weapons.

'We're doomed!' wailed Aars. 'We're all doomed!'

'Cool it, Tin Man,' said Elon. 'I have a plan to get us out of here. A plan of great subtlety and complexity.'

'Thank God,' said Gurk. 'I was worried you were gonna open fire and make a desperate, foolhardy run for the ship.'

There was an awkward silence. Then, with a yell, Elon raised his gun, blasting two guards and the ambassador.

Moments later, the three companions were running pell-mell down the corridor. Death followed in the form of a dozen Vornax troops. Emerging into the hangar, they dodged a volley of sizzling plasma bolts to run up the ramp.

'Learn to shoot, you cephalopod cucks!' Elon shouted as his vehicle took off. It was an epic clap-back from the ultimate shit-poster.

'Watch out!' cried Gurk. 'They're sealing the entrance!'

Icarus 1 tore out of the Vornax hangar just as its aperture closed. Soon they were cruising over New Jersey, some thirty miles from the mother ship. Gurk and Aars looked traumatised, despite being a mutant and a robot respectively.

'Y'know,' said Elon, 'that could have gone a lot worse.'

4

A GRIM DECLARATION

'You did *what*?' cried President Biden, eyes bulging behind his aviators.

Elon sighed, resentful at having to explain himself.

'I shot his son, okay? It was a high-pressure situation and the guy looked at me funny. What do you think I am, some kind of monk?'

Never one to stand up to a billionaire, Biden adopted an emollient tone: 'You're a good boy, Elon, I know you did your best. And I love you, my word as a Biden. But we need to fix this thing. We gotta talk to these Vornax fellas, get them round the table. Serve some pretzels, maybe a hot fudge sundae. Man, the best sundae I ever had was back in '59. Place called Holsten's. I was on a date with this girl, Ruby Mallard. She had a leg for each foot, if you catch my drift, and I was trying to take that poodle skirt for a walk. I apologise, I shouldn't have said that . . .'

Feeling like a grandson trapped in a nursing home, Musk pressed on. 'Look, Mr President, mistakes were made. But trust me, this isn't the end of the world.'

Peterson the aide burst into the Oval Office, a cold sweat on his brow. 'Sir, you ought to see this.'

He switched on a gigantic TV installed by former President Trump. The screen was filled with a close-up shot of King Klathu's face.

'Jeez!' exclaimed Biden. 'That guy looks like Freddy Krueger had a baby with a seafood platter!'

Peterson shook his head in awe. 'This is being broadcast to every device on the planet. Vornax technology is beyond anything we've seen.'

'Meh,' said Elon, 'they're not so hot. I could do that if I wanted.'

Onscreen, Klathu gripped the translation orb, addressing seven billion humans.

'Mankind must answer for this unprovoked attack on our people. As such, I will return to Vornax Prime and raise an armada to conquer your planet. Prepare for subjugation. Resistance is futile.'

'My God!' moaned Peterson, his face draining of all colour. 'So we're to be slaves, the playthings of alien overlords!'

'Listen, Jack,' said Biden, 'just get me in a room with this guy. I'll shake him by the hand or whatever he has going on. Look him straight in the eye. Tell him I understand: he's a Vornax, I'm Irish. We've both faced discrimination. When my family, the O'Bidens, came to this country, they had to work as furniture for rich folks. John D. Rockefeller would use my grandaddy as a footstool, God bless him. So, man, I feel their pain.' Elon shook his head. 'Negotiation is pointless. These savages can't be reasoned with.'

'There is one way humanity can avoid this fate,' King Klathu intoned. 'If Elon Musk issues an apology, we will leave in peace.'

Biden and Peterson looked at Elon imploringly.

The tech lord shrugged. 'Sorry, but I don't apologise.'

'C'mon, man!' said the president. 'Just a tweet. "Sorry, Klathu." We can work with that.'

'Nope,' said Elon, 'not my style.'

'So what am I meant to do?' asked Biden. 'Man, maybe I should give this to Kamala, let her take the heat . . .'

Elon drew himself up to his full six foot two. Arms akimbo, he looked virile and heroic. 'Here's what happens. I jump in my ship and travel to Vornax Prime. Take the fight to our enemy before they have a chance to strike. If I can blow up their armada, that buys us months, maybe years, to build up Earth's defences.'

Peterson looked miserable. Even Biden's faith in Musk seemed shaken.

'I dunno, man,' groused the president. 'Sounds like a mighty tall order . . .'

'Joe, listen to me,' urged Elon. 'I have a foolproof plan to reach the Andromeda Galaxy. All I need is your say-so. And another hundred billion. Please: I'm the only man who can save us.'

Biden sighed. This meeting had interrupted nap-time, and his 4 p.m. chocolate ice cream seemed impossibly far off.

'All right, Musk,' he said. 'The US government will give you our unconditional support. On one condition.'

'Which is?'

'You've gotta take somebody with you. Another guy who knows a thing or two about space.'

Elon winced in trepidation. 'Who?'

Biden pressed a button on his desk. 'Mrs Landingham, could you send in our guest?'

'Who?' Elon repeated.

Biden grinned. 'I chose you for this mission because you're the world's richest man. That means you have a good chance of sorting things out. But the world's *two* richest men? They're certain to succeed.'

Elon stared at the president, mouth agape. 'No. Not him . . .'

A door opened and into the Oval Office strode Jeff Bezos, his bald pate shining.

'Hello, Elon,' said Bezos. 'Long time no see.

I guess we can't all take a five-year vacation on Mars.'

Musk's face reddened. 'Back off, Jeff. I have everything under control.'

'*Au contraire*,' the Amazon magnate purred. 'You're a smart man, Elon, but you're a dreamer. Earth needs someone who can *deliver*.'

5

VOYAGE TO THE UNKNOWN

There was no love lost between Elon Reeve Musk and Jeffrey Preston Bezos. The two had been rivals for years, continually leapfrogging each other in net worth. Though he would never admit it, Elon was intimidated by Jeff, whose Blue Origin provided real competition for SpaceX. For his part, Jeff resented Elon's charisma, his inventiveness, and his lustrous head of hair (which, again, was 100 per cent natural). Before Musk had decamped to Mars, the pair would often spot each other at society balls, yacht parties or private-island gettogethers. When they did, they would invariably fall into childish squabbling and oneupmanship. Elon had once snuck into Jeff's hotel room as the mogul slept and used a permanent marker to write 'number two' on his pate.

Now, though, the pair stood side by side, observing preparations for lift-off at Musk Mission Control. *Icarus 1* was on the launchpad, being optimised for interstellar travel. Technicians scurried about, making adjustments. These were Musk acolytes, demographically identical to his online fanbase. As they worked, they exchanged hilarious references: 'It's a trap!', 'The cake is a lie!', 'I'm Pickle Rick!'

Elon signalled to a passing nerd. 'Make sure to calibrate my antennae. I don't want to lose touch while I'm out there.'

'Yes, sir!' the geek replied, his voice breaking at the excitement of being addressed.

Bezos cast an eye over Mission Control, taking in its rocket silos, coolant system and state-of-the-art command hub.

'I must admit, Elon, you have an impressive set-up here. It's like one of my fulfilment centres, but with fewer bottles of urine.'

'Please,' Elon huffed. 'This is a little more

complex than posting someone a hula hoop made in Guangzhou.'

Anger flickered in Jeff's eyes. 'Look, Musk,' said the bald billionaire, 'I don't like you and you don't like me. But what happens on this mission will determine humanity's future. So what do you say? Truce?'

Bezos held out his hand. Elon considered it.

'Truce.'

The pair shook. To Elon's surprise, after years of bitter rivalry, it felt good to work together. Perhaps they could even be friends, if Jeff were to acknowledge Elon as his intellectual superior.

Gurk lumbered past with a crate of weapons bound for the *Icarus*. He carried it into the ship's hold, beside which stood Aars.

'Attention!' cried the android. 'T-minus one hour to lift-off!'

Just then, another robot approached Musk and Bezos. Unlike Aars, this automaton was female. She had golden skin, scarlet, bow-shaped lips and two metallic cones on her chest. When she spoke, it was with the breathy voice of Marilyn Monroe.

'Hey, Jeffy, can I get you a drink for the flight?'

'No, I'm good, sweetheart.'

Elon couldn't help but ogle her curves. He was a red-blooded male, after all, and she was one sexy robot. Noting his interest, Bezos grinned lasciviously.

'Captain, meet the last member of our crew. This is my gynoid assistant, Alexa.'

T

Sometime later, *Icarus 1* was rocketing through the heavens, a hundred million miles from Earth. Elon expertly fingered the throttles, navigating safely around the asteroid belt. Gurk was in the co-pilot seat, which had a hole specially cut out for his tail. Behind them sat Jeff Bezos and Alexa, who provocatively crossed and uncrossed her legs, *Basic Instinct*-style.

Elon glanced back at them. 'By my calculations, we should reach Andromeda within twenty-four hours. This thing has autopilot, so we can get a little shut-eye.'

'Twenty-four hours?' Bezos repeated, incredulous. 'Even you can't travel 2.5 million light years that fast.'

'Wrong,' Elon shot back. 'For a long time, I've been searching for lithium deposits on other planets. A few months ago, my telescopes discovered a wormhole out by Saturn. I sent in a probe. Can you guess where it emerged?'

'Andromeda,' said Jeff, with grudging admiration.

'Bingo. The Vornax won't know what hit them. Using this wormhole, we can appear right in their backyard.'

T

Twenty-three hours later, the yellow-brown expanse of Saturn loomed before them. Elon swung his ship below the famous rings and pointed its nose towards the wormhole. There it was, wreathed in swirling blue light: the passage to a different galaxy.

'Behold!' said Elon. 'The speculative structure known as an Einstein–Rosen Bridge. Or, as I like to call it, a Musk Hole. Fasten your seatbelts.'

He pulled his control lever back. With a tremendous flare of its quantum engine, *Icarus 1* surged forth and vanished.

6

A BAR IN THE
ANDROMEDA GALAXY

The ship spun uncontrollably, sucked through a vacuum of distorted space-time at inconceivable speed. Its aluminium walls juddered and warped, as though they might rend at any moment. While the others yelled and Gurk barked in terror, Elon gripped the arms of his chair, willing his pulse to remain steady. Then, as quickly as this cosmic maelstrom had engulfed them, it subsided. Now they were sailing on a different sea of stars. Elon finally exhaled.

'Welcome to Andromeda.'

Jeff Bezos grabbed a paper bag and was explosively, protractedly sick. Once finished, he shot

Elon an admiring look. 'Kudos,' he said. 'You actually did it: intergalactic travel!'

Musk was thrilled by the approbation, but acted cool. 'I always knew it would work. Even when the whole scientific community said flying into a wormhole was suicide.'

'Wait, what?'

'And that, if we survived, the radiation would make us sterile and take decades off our lives.'

'Sorry, did you just say sterile?'

Musk turned away, focussing on the task at hand. 'Gurk, set a course for Vornax Prime.'

BOOM! The ship was rocked by a fearful, resounding blast. Alarms blared and red lights flashed.

'What the hell was that?' cried Jeff Bezos.

'I have no idea,' said Elon. 'Aars, damage report!'

The emotional android flapped his arms, panicking. 'Sir, there's been a critical malfunction! My censors indicate electrical fires in the engine room!'

'Then put them out, goddammit!'

'I'll help,' said Jeff, grabbing an extinguisher and rushing after Aars.

'What's going on?' Elon exclaimed. 'I designed *Icarus 1* personally. It's not like one of my products to randomly catch fire.'

Gurk read a flashing display screen, his half-canine features apprehensive. 'This is bad, Mr Musk. If we can't find somewhere to land, the engine's gonna give out. I don't want to be marooned in space. What about my twin loves of literature and chasing after cars?'

'Fear not, my part-animal amigo,' said Elon. 'I just scanned this quadrant and there's a small planet nearby. It's barely inhabited, but it's better than nothing.'

T

And so the *Icarus* crash-landed on the dwarf planet Blarn – Aars gleaned this name from radio transmissions. Its landscape was grey and barren, and its atmosphere rasped the throat. Nonetheless, Elon's crew were able to breathe a sigh of relief and attend to the freak fire. Within the bowels of the ship, Jeff Bezos directed Elon's attention to a scorched section of the quantum engine.

'This is where it started. Shrapnel suggests some kind of explosion.'

Elon peered inside and frowned. 'The engine should be easy enough to mend. But we're going to need new promethium crystals.'

'I'm guessing those are hard to come by.'

'On Earth, yes. Out here, who knows? Our scanners are showing a settlement nearby. I suggest we go mix with the locals and find one who can sell us promethium.'

Bezos's brow furrowed. 'Wait a minute . . . You want to do business with aliens? What if they won't accept Earth currency?'

'Don't worry,' said Elon, 'I brought some of my Bored Ape NFTs. Those are valuable whatever planet you come from.'

T

Leaving Gurk and Alexa to guard the ship, Elon, Jeff and Aars made for the settlement. The humans wore masks to filter the harsh Blarnian air (and in case there was Covid here too). Soon they reached a meagre mining colony that was inhabited by aliens of all shapes and sizes. While Elon did not know their species or understand their tongues, most were engaged in activities familiar to any Earthling. Travelling salesmen pushed carts, vendors hawked their wares and gamblers played strange games in back alleys. A group of inebriated fish-men were gathered around a hole-in-the-wall whose sign consisted of bizarre hieroglyphs. It did not take a seasoned galactic explorer to recognise the place for what it was: a seedy dive bar.

Elon indicated the boozer to his companions. 'That's where we'll find our crystals.'

'Sir!' trilled Aars. 'You can't mean that den of vice!'

'We go where the people are.'

Bezos looked sceptical. 'How are we meant to communicate? I know English and a bit of Spanish, but I have a feeling that won't be enough.'

Elon opened a pouch on his utility belt and produced a glowing red crystal.

'Just show them promethium,' he said. 'They should get the idea. Otherwise, do what you would with any foreigner: loudly repeat yourself until they understand.'

T

The billionaires and the robot walked into the bar. It was a fetid, ramshackle space, thronging with scum and villainy. Creatures with multiple heads, or no head at all, drank nameless liquids. To one side, a pair of hulking, four-armed brutes had a fist fight. At the back of the room was an elevated stage, on which a band played some form of alien jazz.

'Gosh,' said Elon, 'this place is like the Mos Eisley Cantina from *Star Wars*, but just different enough to avoid copyright infringement.'

The frantic tune came to an end, eliciting a tepid round of applause.

'All right,' said Bezos, 'let's see if any of these freaks have what we need.'

Jeff and Aars each took a crystal and went off into the crowd. Elon was about to follow suit when he heard something that stopped him in his tracks. It was music, high-pitched and sublime; the kind of music he imagined being played in heaven, if the angels ditched their harps and got super into synth. Heart in his mouth, Elon turned to see . . .

7

THE SPACE PRINCESS

On the stage where the jazz band had been stood a woman. All of her physiological traits were human, but together, they formed something unmistakably alien. She was the most beautiful person Elon had ever seen, yet this was only the second most remarkable thing about her. For when she sang, it was in a sweet, gossamer voice that shook him to his core. How could a creature of flesh and blood produce sounds so poignant, so ethereal?

Gently swaying on the spot, he heard the following lyrics:

Oooooooh . . .
Oooooooh . . .

Waiting for my spaceman
To take me awaaaaaay.
Out in the spiral arms
That's where we'll plaaaaaay.
Dancing cheek to cheek
In a supernoooooooova.
Love spanning time and space
Will never be oooooo-ver.

Eventually the song reached a climax, and this captivating chanteuse spoke into her microphone: 'Thank you so much. I've been Grimes, goodnight!'

Elon was appalled by the lazy smattering of applause that followed. Had these godless creatures heard what he had? As the singer descended the stage, he bounded up to greet her.

'Hey, Grimes? I've got to say something to you. Your song touched me in a way I've never felt before.'

The other-worldly warbler rolled her eyes. 'Gee, that's great. Don't forget to tip your waiter.'

She tried to move on, but Elon blocked her way.

'Perhaps I could buy you a drink? I have some Bored Apes burning a hole in my pocket.'

Grimes sighed. She'd been around the block and encountered many an alien Lothario. Still, a free drink was a free drink. 'Sure, I can spare a few minutes.'

Together, the technologist and the musician walked over to the bar. Elon watched as obscure spirits were poured into bubbling, vaporiferous goblets.

'I don't suppose these guys serve Budweiser . . .'

T

Elon and Grimes sat in a booth, sipping a pair of Corvengian Martinis. She regarded him with a jaundiced eye.

'So, honey, what brings you to Blarn Town?'

'My ship needs repairs,' said Elon. 'Hang on, this town on the planet Blarn is called Blarn Town?'

'That's right. Makes sense for the only town on this desolate rock. I guess the environment doesn't inspire creativity.'

Now that he was up close, Musk noticed another feature of Grimes's physiology. Every few minutes, her hair would change colour. In the time they had been together, it had passed from lemon to fuchsia to electric blue. She caught him looking.

'I'm Kanadan,' the singer explained. 'It alters depending on my mood.'

'I see,' said Elon. 'And what colour does it go when I charm you?'

She smiled, tight-lipped. 'Cute. So what's your species? Dimnath? Sporb?'

'Human. From planet Earth.'

'Never heard of it.'

There followed a lull in the conversation, so Elon asked something that had been on his mind. 'How is it I understand you? All these other aliens talk gibberish.'

Grimes pointed to a minute mark on her neck, similar to a vaccination scar.

'Universal translator chip, implanted at birth. Ironic, huh? I can communicate in a billion different languages, but I never found a guy worth talking to.'

'Until today,' said Elon, teasing. 'That kind of tech must cost a pretty penny. I'm guessing you grew up rich?'

As a rule, Grimes didn't reveal personal details. But for some reason – perhaps the Corvengian vodka – she felt compelled to tell this strange man the truth.

'You could say that. I wasn't always Grimes, you see. I was born Princess Grimeena of House Booshay, heir to the Kanadan throne. My upbringing was idyllic – long, happy hours spent in the music room – until my father was deposed in a revolution. And for what? Just because the people were living in abject poverty.'

'That's awful,' Elon sympathised. 'I hate when normies think they should be in charge of their lives. Why not let exceptional people decide the big issues, like free speech or what planet we live on?' Grimes continued: 'When the revolutionaries took the palace, they vaporised everyone. My friends, my family, my vocal coach. I was the only one to escape. I chose Blarn as my hiding place, somewhere the Kanadan Revolutionary Council would never look. Ever since then, I've been stuck on this rock, singing at gin joints to make ends meet. I went from Grimeena of House Booshay to plain old Grimes.'

Looking at the wondrous princess, so tough and yet so vulnerable, Elon felt a surge within him. Was it the alien hooch, or something else?

'That's a sad story,' he said. 'Maybe I could help. I happen to be the richest man on my planet.'

Grimes scoffed. 'Listen, hon, I've met a bunch of flashy guys, and they all just wanted one thing. I don't see how you're any different.'

Elon felt momentarily defeated. Then a thought occurred. 'Wait: you're in hiding, under threat of death?'

'Right.'

'So why tell a stranger your life story?'

Grimes paused and, for the first time, smiled with warmth. 'I guess you must have charmed me.'

Musk noted her hair's current shade.

'Silver, then.'

The air between them seemed charged with

potential. Alas, that charge dissipated when Bezos plonked into the booth, followed by Aars.

'Yo, Elon,' said Jeff, 'good news on the crystal front. We found a Blarnite miner who can hook us up.'

Before Musk could respond, Bezos turned to his companion. 'I didn't realise you'd made a friend. Who might you be, my dear?'

'This is Grimes,' murmured Elon, embarrassed by Jeff's obvious flirtation.

'*Enchantée*,' said Bezos, taking Grimes's hand and kissing it, to her visible discomfort. Elon shot him a disapproving look.

'What?' said Jeff. 'Since the split with Mac-Kenzie, I've been single and ready to mingle. Can't I have a little fun?'

Grimes stood abruptly, adjusting her lavender hair.

'Excuse me, I should get back to my dressing room. Nice meeting you, Elon.'

A helpless Musk watched the vision depart. Once she was gone, he rounded on Bezos. 'What the hell, Jeff? I was making a real connection!'

'Oh, I'm sorry,' snarked Bezos, 'is our mission to save humanity getting in the way of your love life?'

'I'm sorry, sir,' said Aars, 'but I must agree with Master Jeff. Our prime directive is to reach the Vornax home-world.'

'Fine,' Musk muttered, downing his cocktail. 'Let's get back to the ship.'

Jeff and Aars headed for the exit. Elon followed ruefully, certain he would never see Grimes again.

8

A DARING RESCUE

A Rodarian fruit-seller glanced up from the xilph berries he was sorting. Near his stall had gathered a group of sinister men, humanoid in appearance and clad entirely in black. While their faces were masked, their hair was visible, shifting through a succession of hues. Had the Rodarian been better acquainted with the Inner Rim, he might have recognised them as Kanadans. More specifically, they were agents of the Kanadan Revolutionary Council, and on their minds was murder.

Tenogg, the unit's leader, addressed his subordinates: 'Intelligence indicates the princess is in that bar. Our mission is to storm the building, apprehend the royal and take her back to Kanada for show trial and execution. If any sentients try to intervene, terminate them with extreme prejudice.'

Quarm, his lieutenant, looked uncomfortable. 'Captain, are we sure about this? When the revolution happened, she was but a child.'

In one liquid motion, Tenogg unsheathed his vibro-blade and slashed Quarm's throat. Gurgling, the lieutenant collapsed. Tenogg glared at his remaining men. 'Grimeena's father cast my entire family into a black hole. They received no mercy, and neither will she. For the revolution!'

The agents of the KRC erupted in a wild cheer. Drawing their own vibro-blades, they charged into the bar.

T

Grimes was in her dressing room, removing the last of her stage make-up. She met her reflection's eye and frowned. Years ago, when her family and friends were taken from her, she had sworn off emotional connection. So why couldn't she stop thinking of the strange Earthman she met an hour ago? Sure, he was an alluring, muscular Adonis, but that hardly accounted for her interest. What beguiled her was the blazing intellect behind those eyes. Enough, she thought, it's not like you'll ever see him again. Her hair settled into turquoise, the colour of thwarted passion.

CRASH! The dressing-room door came off its hinges as a phalanx of revolutionaries poured in. Grimes stood and turned to face them, her eyes impossibly huge.

'Oh my goodness, who are you? What on Blarn do you want?'

Tenogg stepped forward, removing his mask to reveal a scarred, scowling face. 'By order of the Kanadan Revolutionary Council, I arrest you, Grimeena of House Booshay. We will return to Kanada, where you are to stand trial.'

Grimes put a hand to her chest, adopting an expression of unimpeachable innocence. 'Who, me? But I'm just a singer in a dive bar.'

'Your class is full of deceit,' growled Tenogg. 'While you roam free, the revolution will never be safe.'

He motioned to one of his men, who went

to grab her, vibro-blade in hand. A purple light flashed, accompanied by a crackle of energy and a rush of hot air. The KRC soldier fell backwards, bisected at the waist. Horrified, Tenogg looked from his slain comrade to Princess Grimeena. There was a blade in her hand, too: a burning laser sword. Her hair had turned from turquoise to a deep red. This meant war.

'You really think I fled the palace without visiting Dad's armoury?'

Grimes expertly twirled her sword, assuming an offensive stance. 'Now, which of you commie scumbags is next?'

T

On *Icarus 1*, Elon finished installing the new crystals. He called up to Gurk in the cockpit. 'Ignite!'

'Aye, Captain!' responded the semi-canine.

Naturally, his adjustments had done the trick: the engine flared to life. Elon returned to the cockpit and and flopped in his chair. 'Promethium crystals functioning at 100 per cent.'

'Great,' said Jeff Bezos. 'Time to get off this hellhole.'

Elon gave an absent nod. He was thinking of the princess in the dive bar. For reasons even he, a rational genius, couldn't explain, it felt as though they had unfinished business. Like their fates were subtly but irrevocably entwined. Banishing such mumbo-jumbo from his prodigious mind, he retracted the landing gears and blasted off.

T

The *Icarus* made its ascent, swooping over the dingy streets of Blarn Town. As he twiddled the flux capacitor, Elon saw something from the corner of his eye: a disturbance in the square they had visited earlier. Whipping out his trusty electron binoculars, he focused on the source of the commotion. It was Grimes, wielding a purple laser sword and being chased by a group of thugs! Now they had her surrounded, ten against one!

Yanking the controls, Elon spun his ship 180 degrees.

Bezos nearly fell from his seat. 'What are you doing?' he yelped. 'Why are we going back?'

'Unfinished business.'

T

The Rodarian fruit-seller watched with horror as KRC agents crept towards the princess, vibro-blades humming. Two of them charged with ululating battle cries. She struck down one and then the other, sparks flying from the laser sword. A valiant effort, but she remained outnumbered, and a single blow could be the end of her. Tenogg raised a hand and his commandos halted. He approached Grimes, brandishing his blade with lethal dexterity.

'Perhaps we should skip your trial and go straight to execution.'

Grimes had learned to fight on the mean streets of Blarn Town. She was more than capable of handling herself. However, this man was a lifelong soldier and remorseless killer. She braced herself for the coming onslaught . . .

PEW! PEW-PEW-PEW! Tenogg was suddenly riddled with laser bolts. His men dived for cover as shots from above pierced their body armour and exploded their heads. A couple of strays hit the Rodarian's fruit stall, incinerating his precious xilph berries. Alas, such were the casualties of war. Bewildered but relieved, Grimes looked for the source of the bolts. Elon Musk, wearing a jet-pack, floated to the ground and holstered his twin blasters.

'My God,' said Grimes, 'you're the guy from the bar. What are you doing here?'

'I saw you were in trouble, so I thought I'd drop in. Fancy a ride?'

Grimes glanced at the surviving KRC agents, who were beginning to regroup. 'Why not? I've been meaning to blow this popsicle stand.'

She jumped into Elon's arms as he activated the jetpack's engines. Together they shot upwards, towards the *Icarus* and freedom.

T

Once they were safely in the ship's hold, Elon set Grimes down. 'Welcome aboard. This is my ship, *Icarus 1.*'

The space princess gazed on the Earthman with newfound respect. 'That was some sharp shooting back there.'

'Thanks,' said Elon. 'You're pretty handy with that sword.'

Piloted by Gurk, the vehicle was now leaving Blarn's atmosphere. Grimes marvelled at this reversal of fortune: one moment she was about to die, the next she was escaping her planetary prison.

'Elon, you saved my life. How can I ever repay you?'

The dashing adventurer ran his fingers through his hair.

'Well, we could use a navigator. We're trying to get to Vornax Prime, and you're familiar with this star system.'

'Sure, I can get you there,' said Grimes. 'The Vornax planet is a couple of days away.'

Elon smiled. 'Good. Then we have plenty of time to get to know each other . . .'

9

LOVE AMONG THE STARS

Elon Musk was in the *Icarus*'s workshop, tinkering with one of his brilliant inventions. This was his magnum opus, even greater than that giant straw to suck Thai schoolboys out of a cave. The flame of an oxy-acetylene torch reflected in his goggles, which looked super masculine and cool. Hearing a knock at the door, he turned off the fire and pulled up his protective eyewear.

'Come in!'

It was Grimes, her hair a fetching lime green. 'Hey,' she said, somewhat tentative. 'What you up to?'

'I'm working on a super-secret, 100 per cent awesome project,' he replied. 'You're from another planet, so you probably haven't heard of Marvel Studios, but I'm basically the real-life Tony Stark.'

'Nice. Well, sorry to disturb you.'

'Not at all.'

He threw a tarp over his invention, removed his goggles and welding apron, and gestured to a nearby bunk. The pair sat on the narrow bed.

'Anything I can do for you?'

It was then he realised that Grimes's big, anime eyes were full of tears. She wiped them angrily, loath to show weakness. 'Gah . . . I guess my run-in with those KRC agents rattled me. I could sure use some company.'

'I'm excellent company,' said Elon. 'I've memorised every Monty Python routine, and I have strong feelings about *Zach Snyder's Justice League.* Want me to sing you a Weird Al song?'

'Perhaps you could tell me about Ulf.'

'Ulf?'

'Your home planet.'

'Oh, *Earth.* Yeah, it's pretty chill – there's lots of lithium, which you can use to make cool cars. But

I always dreamed of transcending my birthplace. Wandering the stars, conquering new realms. I'm not content to be the world's richest and smartest man. My life's work is to render mankind an inter-planetary species.'

Grimes wondered at this odd man who spoke with such zeal. 'So you're a leader of your people? You must be very popular.'

'Oh yeah, everyone respects me. Literally every-one. I'm renowned for my business acumen, my tech savvy, my quick-fire wit. Plus, I've dated a string of high-profile hotties. We're talking Amber Heard, Talulah Riley – perfect tens.'

Grimes bit her lower lip and ran a finger through her tangerine hair. 'I must admit, I'm drawn to you. No male has ever had this effect on me.'

'I secrete powerful pheromones,' said Elon. 'It's true of all the men in my family, hence our sur-name.'

Unable to contain her arousal, Grimes drew him into a torrid embrace. Their limbs entwined as their questing tongues explored each other's mouths.

Before long, their clothes were strewn across the workshop like wrapping paper on Christmas morning. They writhed upon the bed, two prizefighters exchanging blows of pure pleasure. The singer discovered new pitches in her vocal range as Elon brought her to one shuddering climax after another. He was a virtuoso, the Itzhak Perlman of intercourse, and the female form was his Stradivarius.

After several hours, the pair lay satiated, wrapped in each other's arms. Grimes basked in her postcoital glow. 'God, I had no idea it could feel like that. You transported me to hidden realms of ecstasy with your panther-like prowess.'

Elon gave a sweaty grin. 'I think I can do better. Ready for round two?'

The lovers merged once more in perfect intimacy. However, unbeknownst to them, a shadowy figure was watching through a peephole. This was no voyeur: his motives were far worse.

'My, my,' murmured Jeff Bezos, 'what do we have here?'

10

THE HIDDEN ENEMY

Back on Earth, the nerds at Musk Mission Control were gathered in the command hub. On a vast screen was projected the face of their idol. He said: 'I am transmitting this video from the Andromeda Galaxy, via wormhole. Pretty cool, huh?'

The nerds agreed vociferously. Though he couldn't hear them, they whooped and hollered, many crying with joy.

'Elon rules!' 'You're the man, Elon!' 'I would gladly die for you!'

The recording continued: 'In another first, I had sex with an alien.'

The nerds became yet more giddy.

'That's one lucky alien!' 'I'll have sex with you, Elon!'

'Anyway, I should wrap this up. Need to plan the assault on Vornax Prime. But keep believing in me, yeah? Together we can save the world.'

This was too much for a crowd of Musketeers. Half of them gave a standing ovation, while the rest fainted like teenage girls at a Beatles concert. Such was the general euphoria that no one noticed the arrival of an Amazon courier, who placed a large parcel in their midst. Eventually, the Mission Control staff calmed down. Returning to work, they amused themselves by swapping references.

'Oh my God, you killed Kenny!' said Nerd 1. '*South Park.*'

'Uh, phrasing?' said Nerd 2. '*Archer.*'

After some time had passed, one of them finally noticed the mysterious parcel. It sat on the main terminal, emitting a faint, rhythmic noise. Tick, tick, tick . . .

'What's in the box?!' cried Nerd 1. 'Brad Pitt, *Se7en.*'

'Danger, Will Robinson, danger!' replied Nerd 2. 'Robbie the Robot, *Lost in Space.*'

Nerd 1 got up from his gaming chair and approached the Amazon package. Before he could open it, another video appeared on the big screen. This time, it was the cruel, hairless face of Jeff Bezos.

'Hello, virgins,' Bezos gloated. 'I bet you're wondering why I sent you a gift. Well, I have plans for your beloved Elon, and I don't want him radioing for help. So enjoy the present. After all, it cost . . . *a bomb.*'

His heart sinking, Nerd 1 opened the package to find fifty pounds of C4.

'Oh, I've wasted my life,' he said. 'Comic Book Guy, *The Simpsons.*'

KA-BOOM! The C4 ignited, obliterating the building and killing every nerd inside.

T

On *Icarus 1*, the crew had gathered in the ship's communal area. This included Grimes, who was now officially part of the mission. Jeff chatted to

Alexa, while Gurk spun in circles trying to catch his own tail. Aars, ever the worrywart, took Elon aside.

'Sir, by introducing a new member to the crew, we increase our risk profile by twenty-three per cent.'

'Aars, don't sweat it. Not that you can sweat. Point is, I trust her.'

'But why, sir?'

Elon smirked. 'Let's just say I have insider info.'

Aars sighed. 'I'll never understand you humans.'

They walked over to the rest of the group.

'Okay, folks,' Elon announced, 'we'll be reaching Vornax Prime in approximately twelve hours. Our mission is to destroy the Vornax fleet before it can threaten Earth.'

'And how exactly do we do that?' asked Bezos.

Musk shrugged. 'We improvise.'

'That hardly fills me with confidence.'

'Well, it should, given my super-genius powers.'

'Elon's right,' said Grimes. 'Of course he'll think of something: he's the smartest man on Ulf.'

Her tone was passionate. Bezos raised an eyebrow. 'You two seem to be getting along. I suppose space travel makes strange bedfellows . . .'

Elon brushed past this. 'In the meantime, everyone should get some rest. Goodnight.'

The group dispersed. Gurk headed to his kennel, Aars to his charging port. Once Elon and Grimes were out of earshot, Bezos placed a hand on the small of Alexa's back.

'I have a task for you, sweetheart . . .'

T

Elon and Grimes had agreed to spend the night apart, preserving their vital energies for the mission. Therefore Elon was alone when he entered his quarters, only to find Alexa posing suggestively on his bed. She wore a skimpy negligee, which was confusing, as she usually didn't wear clothes. It shouldn't have been sexy, and yet . . .

'Hey, Lonny. It's awful cold on this spaceship. Maybe you could warm me up?'

'How can you be cold?' said Elon. 'The thermostat's set to twenty-two degrees. Also, you're a robot.'

Alexa shifted position, pointing her metallic cones straight at him. 'Even robots have needs, baby.'

'You mean software updates, oil changes, new batteries . . . ?'

'I'm saying I want to make love.'

Flustered, Elon stared at his shoes. 'Oh, um, I dunno . . . Maybe we should stay friends? Not that we were friends to begin with. You're more like my arch-rival's android assistant.'

'I can be what you want me to be,' said Alexa.

Her finger whirred as she beckoned him. Feeling his willpower evaporate, Elon went and sat beside her. Temptation and guilt warred within him.

'Let's just talk, okay?'

'Whatever you say,' Alexa purred. 'And while we talk, I can give you a massage.'

Before he could demur, her mechanical hands were doing their work. She found his every knot with inhuman precision. Elon groaned, alarmed at how good it felt.

'Oh, sweetie,' said Alexa, 'you're so tense. I guess

that's how it is for super-geniuses. You have the weight of the world on your shoulders.'

'Mm,' he said. 'No one knows how hard it is to be Elon Musk.'

'Then it's my job to help you relax.'

With that, she pushed Elon onto his back and climbed on top of him. The last of his discipline fading, he allowed himself to succumb. Forget Grimes: he belonged to Alexa. Suddenly, her voice became a harsh, robotic monotone: 'INITIATING FELLATIO SEQUENCE.'

The spell broken, Elon covered his crotch. 'Alexa, stop!'

The gynoid obeyed. 'Everything all right, sugar?'

Elon shook his head. 'I'm sorry, I can't do this. You're a very attractive machine, but my heart belongs to another.'

'Oh. Okay,' said Alexa, and Elon fancied he heard a note of regret in her computer-generated voice.

Just then, the door to his cabin swung open. Through it came Grimes.

'Elon, I couldn't stay away. No one could resist your –'

She froze at the sight of her lover being straddled by a sexbot. In an instant, her hair turned fiery red. Elon gulped.

'Darling! It's not what it looks like!'

She responded in the imperious tone of one who grew up royal. 'Oh, isn't it? Cos it looks like you're betraying me with a cyber-slut.'

'Hey!' cried Alexa. 'Lonny, are you gonna let her call me that?'

Elon pushed the gynoid off him. For once, he found himself lost for words. 'I – I – I . . .' he spluttered.

'You know what?' said Grimes. 'I don't even care. I slept with you because I thought maybe – just maybe – you were different from other men. That you cared about my electro-pop compositions, not just my body. But now I see you're nothing but a sleazy space cowboy. Goodbye, Elon.'

'Grimes, wait!'

She withdrew, slamming the door behind her. Elon put his head in his hands. The first profound connection he had made with a woman, and he threw it all away! Alexa patted him on the shoulder. 'Still wanna do stuff?'

There was a long pause.

'. . . No.'

11

ELON'S GAMBIT

The voice of Aars blared through the ship's speakers. 'Attention! We have entered the star system containing Vornax Prime. Please report to the canteen.'

Elon sighed and rose from his bunk. Normally he would have been thrilled to leap headfirst into adventure. However, after the events of last night, he hardly felt like a hero. Being caught in flagrante with Alexa was the most embarrassed he'd been since his appearance on *The Joe Rogan Experience*. And, much like pulling a dorky face while smoking a joint, this couldn't be undone. He wondered if Grimes would ever forgive him. Alas, defending humanity from alien subjugation was proving less fun than he had hoped.

T

A few minutes later, he slunk into the canteen and took his rations, doing his best to avoid Grimes's gaze. Jeff Bezos glanced up from a bowl of space-porridge and grinned.

'Trouble in paradise?'

Beside the e-commerce tycoon sat Alexa, looking as miserable as her immobile face would allow.

'Leave it, Jeff,' sighed Elon. 'This is a big day: I don't have time for your jibes.'

As he munched his space-granola, a disturbing thought occurred to Elon. Alexa worked for Bezos. Might it follow that she made her seduction attempt at his behest? And, if so, why? Such a move was likely to create tension and disunity among the crew. Could that somehow benefit Jeff?

No, thought Elon, you're being ridiculous. Occam's razor: the simplest explanation is usually correct. Alexa wanted to sleep with you because you're hot as hell. Sure, she's a robot, but she's a female robot, and thus receptive to your charms. You should forget these conspiracy theories and focus on the mission.

As if to underscore this, Aars burst into the canteen, waving his arms. 'Sir! Sir! It's a disaster! Oh, what will become of us?'

Elon jumped to his feet. 'What's the matter, Aars?'

'It's the Vornax. They're on high alert, scanning the entire quadrant for hostile spacecraft.'

'Hmm,' mused Elon. 'It's as if they knew we were coming . . . But how?'

'Sounds like there's no getting through,' said Jeff Bezos. 'I guess we should go home. It's a shame, because I was really up for defeating those guys.'

'Negative,' said Musk. 'There must be some way to evade detection. To the cockpit!'

T

The crew of *Icarus 1* gathered around a holographic map of the Vornax system.

'There,' said Elon, pointing at a torus of celestial debris.

'The asteroid belt?' asked Bezos. 'What of it?'

'If we approach Vornax Prime directly, we show up on their scanners and get blown to smithereens. But if we come at them through the asteroids . . .'

'. . . they won't be able to detect us until it's too late,' Grimes finished.

Elon glanced up, making eye contact with her for the first time that day. 'Exactly.'

'Just one problem,' said Bezos. 'We need a computer to chart our way through. This ship doesn't have anywhere near the processing power.'

'That's what Mission Control's for.'

Elon went to the broadcast terminal and sent the nerds a detailed map of the asteroid belt. An hour later, there had been no response.

'It doesn't make sense,' said Elon. 'Those guys hang on my every word. Something must have happened . . .'

'In any case,' said Bezos, 'we're screwed. Maybe we should just surrender to the Vornax.'

'Never!' cried Elon, striking a gallant pose.

'You're forgetting one key detail: I'm the universe's greatest pilot. I don't need a computer to fly.'

Aars panicked, sparks shooting out of his ears. 'Sir, the chances of successfully navigating an asteroid field are approximately 3,720 to 1!'

Elon grinned cockily. 'I like those odds.'

'No way,' Bezos protested. 'I won't allow it.'

'My ship, my rules,' said Musk.

'I never agreed to that.'

'How about a democratic vote?' suggested Grimes.

The two billionaires considered it.

'Fine,' said Bezos. 'But his robot can't vote.'

'Neither can his,' Elon shot back.

'And Gurk has dog IQ, so he should sit this one out. No offence, Gurk.'

'None taken, Mr Bezos. Arf!'

'All right,' said Elon, 'humans only. I say we fly through the asteroids.'

'I vote for going home,' said Bezos. He turned to Grimes expectantly. 'You're the tiebreaker. Come on, are you really going to put your life in this guy's hands?'

There came a long pause.

'If Elon says he can get us through in one piece, I believe him.'

'Unbelievable!' Bezos threw up his hands and stormed out.

Elon felt a swell of gratitude towards Grimes. 'Thanks for backing me up there.'

She greeted this with a hard expression. 'I did it because you were right, not because I like you.'

Elon's face fell. 'Oh.'

'You saved me back on Blarn,' she continued. 'By Kanadan tradition, I owe you a life debt. But after this mission, we're through.'

With that, Grimes went over to her seat. Elon sunk into his own, downhearted. But there was no time for feminine emotion. Seizing the controls, he steered *Icarus 1* into danger.

T

Like the belt between Mars and Jupiter, these asteroids varied hugely in scale, ranging from around 400 miles in diameter to a mere 10 metres. Unlike

our belt, the space between the rocks was narrow, and collisions were frequent. Elon knew, as he sped towards the maelstrom, that a single ding could be fatal. If some tiny stone punctured their hull, it would expose them to the terrifying void of space. And yet, despite this knowledge, Elon was not afraid. He felt his adrenalin spike as he pulled on his headset. Space acrobatics was his forte, and he made it look good.

As *Icarus* entered the belt, flecks of rock began to clatter against the ship.

'We're going to die!' shrieked Aars. 'We're all going to die!'

Musk rolled his eyes, wondering why he had given the android such an irritating voice. 'Keep your cool, Tin Man,' he said. 'That was the easy part.'

Right on cue, a large rock, some 200 metres across, tumbled in front of them. Elon banked right, scraping a fin as he flew past it. Looping around a couple more boulders, *Icarus 1* moved deep within the danger zone. Now asteroids were coming at them thick and fast. It was even more perilous than Elon had expected, testing his pilot skills to the utmost degree.

'Woof!' cried Gurk. 'Watch out!'

A mid-sized rock hurtled at them, as though launched by catapult. Elon pitched and rolled, escaping destruction by milliseconds. Beads of sweat appeared on his brow. That was far too close.

'Sorry, guys,' he croaked.

To his surprise, a hand squeezed his upper arm. It was Grimes. 'Believe in yourself,' she said. 'You may be a fuckboi, but you're one hell of a pilot.'

Buoyed by this, he executed a series of miraculous manoeuvres, taking them ever closer to safety. But then, disaster: a baseball-sized stone whizzed out of Elon's blindspot. It clipped the *Icarus*'s starboard bow and sent the ship spinning. Musk laboured mightily to stabilise.

'This is it!' Aars keened. 'There is literally no chance of us surviving!'

'Will someone shut him up?' said Grimes, leaping from her chair.

'Where are you going?' Elon demanded.

'I figure you could use some help, cowboy.'

She raced out of the cockpit and climbed into the ship's gun turret. Powering up the photon cannons, she spoke into her comms unit. 'Time to clear you some space.'

Grimes gripped the controls, hooking her finger around the trigger. BLAM BLAM BLAM! With perfect aim, she hit every asteroid that threatened them, either knocking them off course or exploding them into dust. Seeing his chance, Elon zigged and zagged through the rubble.

'Grimes,' he yelled, 'check your six!'

She pivoted the turret 180 degrees and blasted the slab that had been coming up behind them.

'Very nice!' said Elon.

Corkscrewing through a tight cluster of 'roids, he scented victory. 'We're almost out of the woods . . .'

'Don't speak too soon,' said Grimes.

Then Elon saw them. Two gigantic asteroids loomed either side of the ship, converging like a pair of tectonic plates.

'Oh no, we'll be crushed!' cried an inconsolable Aars.

Elon had mere nanoseconds to react. Should he veer upwards? Downwards? Attempt a U-turn? The slightest miscalculation meant death. Coming to a decision, he yanked back the throttle. *Icarus 1* sped to where the asteroids were about to meet.

Gurk, usually impassive, let out a frightened howl. 'Aroo! You're not gonna make it!'

'Watch me.'

The *Icarus* shot, dart-like, along the narrow ravine. On each side, a wall of rock moved closer and closer. Normally, Elon would have observed that this was reminiscent of the trash compactor scene in *Star Wars*, but now was not the time. They had a hundred metres of room. Then fifty. Then twenty. Then five.

Grimes's voice crackled in his headset. 'I hope you know what you're doing.'

Elon gritted his teeth. 'This isn't my first time between a rock and a hard place.'

An instant before the space-mountains collided, *Icarus 1* emerged from the gap. They were now clear of the asteroid belt.

'Whoooooo!' Elon shouted. 'Gurk, did we trigger any sensors?'

'Negative, sir,' panted his co-pilot. 'The Vornax have no idea we're here.'

Aars had fainted, which didn't make much sense for a robot, but everyone was glad of the peace. Grimes re-entered the cockpit, dusting off her hands. Elon glanced over his shoulder, affording her a grin.

'That was some sharpshooting back there.'

The alien princess responded with a minuscule smile of her own. 'I guess we make a decent team. Even if you are a prick.'

It wasn't ideal, but Elon would take it. Feeling rather more heroic than he had an hour ago, he adjusted the controls and *Icarus 1* began its descent. Vornax Prime awaited.

12

BELLY OF THE BEAST

The planet was as hellish close up as it had been from space. Boiling seas. Vast, grey deserts. A scorched and thundering sky. King Klathu had not misled when he spoke of ecological collapse. It was almost unthinkable that this wasteland had once been lush and lively. I should probably get round to fixing Earth's climate, thought Elon.

Cruising at low altitude, the *Icarus* soon came to Vorblagard, capital of Vornax Prime. By far the largest city on the planet, it was jagged with skyscrapers, all hewn from the same dark material as the ship that had menaced New York. While human metropolises teemed with light, this one seemed to absorb it. Elon could swear the place wished to swallow them up. As *Icarus 1* passed over the spiked walls of the city, it flickered out of existence.

'Cloaking device activated,' growled Gurk. 'It won't stand up to heavy scrutiny, but should give us a chance to land undetected.'

'Over there,' said Elon.

In the middle of Vorblagard was an enormous airfield, many miles across. On it stood row after row of colossal battleships, each connected to a central pipeline. Surrounding the whole thing was a 300-foot perimeter wall. This was supplemented by a series of guard towers, from which searchlights shone, ceaselessly scanning the ground.

'Damn,' said Gurk. 'These guys don't skimp on security.'

Elon swooped down, landing *Icarus 1* in a large culvert outside the wall.

T

'So,' said Bezos, 'they have a huge, heavily-guarded armada, no doubt equipped with weaponry beyond human imagination. And our plan is to break in and sabotage this technology we don't understand. Do I have that right?'

Elon didn't like Jeff's tone. Clearly, he was still salty about the asteroid thing. 'Yes.'

'Okay . . . Any idea how we do that? I'm all ears, super-genius.'

Musk tented his fingers, the universal sign that someone is about to say clever shit.

'The Vornax fleet may be advanced, but it clearly runs on some kind of combustible fuel. If we plant thermal detonators along that pipeline, they could cause a chain reaction and take the ships out of commission.'

'Hmm,' said Bezos, 'that just might work. But we'll need a finely honed plan of attack.'

'Way ahead of you,' replied Elon. 'I say we divide into three teams. Grimes and I set the charges. You and Alexa infiltrate that tower and disable their security system. Gurk and Aars will sweep the perimeter, incapacitating as many guards as possible.'

'Whoa whoa whoa,' said Bezos. 'I don't have any combat training, and let's just say Alexa was made for love not war. If you send us out together, we're screwed.'

He gestured at Grimes. 'I should go with Miss Laser Sword.'

Elon growled: 'Listen, Bezos . . .'

'He's right,' said Grimes. 'I'm not happy about it, but his logic is sound.'

'Fine,' said Elon. 'We split up the fighters. Me and Alexa, Grimes and Jeff, Gurk and Aars.'

'Sir!' Aars exclaimed. 'I know you're always correct, but are you sure you want to entrust me to that flea-bitten fur-ball? No offence, Gurk.'

T

Once Aars had calmed down, the group moved to the ship's armoury. Every surface was laden with weapons and gadgets, all the latest in Musk technology. Gurk grabbed his sonic hammer while Jeff fumbled with a raygun.

'I've never used one of these before. Still, how hard can it be?'

Sighing, Elon offered another of his guns to Grimes.

'No, thanks,' she said. 'Blasters are clumsy and random. This –' she held up her sword – 'is an elegant weapon for a more civilised age.'

Needled by Grimes's disregard for his inventions, Musk moved on. 'We should use call signs while we're in the field. Gurk'll be Wolfman. Aars'll be Jeeves. Alexa, you can be Barbie. Grimes, Galadriel. And Jeff, you're Chrome Dome.'

'I demand a better nickname,' said Bezos.

'Sorry,' Elon replied, 'luck of the draw. As for me, I'll be God King.'

He checked his watch, now set to Vornaxian time. 'Okay, let's get this party started. Look alive, people: what we do in the next few hours will determine the rest of history. Back on Earth, there are seven billion people counting on us.'

Yes, thought Jeff Bezos, and I'm counting on you. Counting on you to be your sloppy, oblivious, arrogant self. Soon my master plan will be enacted. Then you will rue the day you knocked me off the Forbes number one spot . . . At the thought of his impending victory, Bezos let out a weird, high-pitched giggle.

Elon, who had been halfway out the room, turned back to him, confused. 'Sorry, did I say something funny?'

'No,' replied Bezos, alarmed. 'I was just thinking of an amusing comedy programme I watched recently.'

'What's it called?' demanded Musk.

Bezos tried to recall a single comedy programme. In truth, he wasn't a fan of laughing: acquisition and logistics were more his speed. He certainly wasn't pop-culture-savvy like Elon, who had done cameos for *The Big Bang Theory* and *Rick and Morty*.

'I forget. But it was on Amazon Prime, an incredible streaming service that everyone should use.'

'Whatever,' said Musk, as he headed for the exit.

13

BETRAYAL ON VORNAX PRIME

The ragtag group emerged from their culvert and, using grappling-hook guns, ascended the airfield's perimeter wall. They rappelled down to the tarmac and hid behind a fuel tank as a searchlight passed over them. Elon opened his haversack to check the thermal detonators. There they were: a series of silver disks that fit in the palm, each with a red, blinking LED at the centre. He looked up at his companions.

'Okay, team, you have your missions. Remember: the only way any of us will succeed is if all of us succeed. God King out!'

The group began to disperse. Before Grimes could leave, Elon placed a hand on her arm.

'Princess,' he said, 'in case anything happens . . . I want to say I'm sorry. The whole thing with Alexa. You deserve better than that.'

She gazed back at him, her eyes softer than before. 'Tell you what,' she said, 'if we survive this, we can have that talk.'

Elon nodded. 'Deal.'

And so, in the heart of darkness, the fellowship set off on their separate quests.

T

Grimes and Bezos moved through the shadows until they reached the airfield's main guard tower. She braced herself for combat as they entered the building, but the cavernous space was empty.

'Something's off,' she observed. 'I thought this guard tower would have guards.'

Bezos shrugged. 'I say we count our blessings. There!'

He indicated a spiral staircase, which the pair proceeded to climb. A hundred or so steps later, they entered a darkly gleaming control room, also deserted.

Grimes frowned, squeezing the hilt of her laser sword. 'This is too easy.'

'Maybe we're just that good,' said Bezos, walking up to a central console. 'Only problem is, I don't read Vornax . . .'

Each button on the console was labelled with what looked like random inkblots.

'I do,' said Grimes. 'See this button? Underneath, it says "deactivate security system".'

'Wow,' said Bezos, 'I don't know why they have that, but I'm not complaining.'

T

From behind the fuel tank, Musk and Alexa watched as the searchlights were suddenly extinguished. Bezos's voice came through on the comms unit. 'Mission accomplished with time to spare. Beat that, Elon.'

'It's God King, Chrome Dome. But well done.'

He turned to Alexa. 'Let's go.'

The coast now clear, they raced across the airfield until they came to the mammoth pipeline that fuelled the Vornax ships. Alexa scanned the area as Elon started placing explosives at critical points along the pipe's underside.

T

Elsewhere, a group of ten Vornax troops were patrolling the perimeter. Seeing something, their leader held up his claw and they halted. He had spotted a flustered 'droid approaching. Aars called out to them.

'Yoo-hoo! Beg your pardon, but I could do with a little help. I got lost looking for the . . . little robots' room.'

The group leader's tentacles undulated moistly. He turned to his men, who were just as baffled as him. So baffled were they, they didn't notice the giant dog-man bounding towards them. WHUMP! With a swing of his sonic hammer, Gurk sent four guards flying. Another two leapt at him, but Aars zapped them with a tranq ray. Working together, Musk's exotic companions made short work of the remaining Vornax. Once they were all immobilised, Gurk stowed their limp forms in a nearby dugout.

'Nice distracting,' said Gurk to Aars.

'How many times are we going to do this?' asked the robot.

'As many as we need. Mr Musk said to clear the area.'

'Oh, I'm not cut out for fighting. I was built to buttle, not battle.'

'And half of me wants to spend all day licking my crotch. We don't get to choose our destiny.'

Gurk suddenly froze and sniffed the air. 'We should move,' he growled. 'I smell more guards approaching.'

He then sniffed in the opposite direction.

'What's happening?' Aars demanded.

'My doggie sense is tingling,' murmured Gurk. 'It's as though there's Vornax all around us.'

'Well, I don't see anything.'

The air around them rippled and warped as a dozen Vornax lowered their invisibility shields. Gurk and Aars were surrounded, hopelessly outgunned.

'We're surrounded!' cried Aars. 'And hopelessly outgunned!'

One of the warriors drew near, bellowing a

series of squelches. He jabbed a clawed finger at Gurk's hammer.

'You want me to drop my weapon?' the man-dog enquired. 'Happy to oblige.'

With that, Gurk brought down his sonic hammer, sending shockwaves through the ground. They knocked the Vornax to the floor and Aars onto his arse. Gurk made a break for it, scooping up his android friend.

'Oh!' cried Aars. 'You scuffed my finish, you maladroit mutt!'

'Would you rather be in the clutches of those squid men? We need to tell Mr Musk they're on to us.'

He whipped out his communicator. 'God King, this is Wolfman. Do you copy, over? I said, do you copy, over?'

The only response was a squall of white noise.

'Oh no!' wailed Aars. 'They're jamming our communications. But how? Someone would have to give them the access codes.'

'Could it be Bezos?' asked the half-hound. 'He seems evil as hell.'

'Jeff Bezos do something reprehensible?' said Aars. 'That's the stupidest thing you've ever said!'

By now the Vornax guards had recovered and were unleashing a fusillade of plasma bolts in their direction.

'In any case,' said Gurk, 'there's only one thing for it. We must return to the ship and await Mr Musk's orders.'

They arrived at a sealed exit. Gurk set Aars down and, with a mighty hammer-blow, knocked the gate clean off its hinges. Dodging yet more bolts, the pair sped through the tunnel and out to freedom.

T

'Done!' said Elon, laying the last of the thermal detonators. A satisfying CLUNK signalled that the bomb's electro-magnet had engaged. It would now be near impossible to pry off the pipe. He turned back to Alexa, who was on lookout, her head slowly rotating 360 degrees.

'Let's go,' he said. 'I'm not keen to be here when things heat up.'

Together they stalked across the darkened airfield. As they moved, Elon spoke into his communicator. 'Musketeers, this is God King. Explosives are in place. Meet me and Alexa at the rendezvous and let's blow this thing.'

Hearing nothing but white noise, Elon looked worried. 'I think there's a comms malfunction. Or else . . .'

Alexa cut him off with a fearful gasp. 'My sensors show a legion of Vornax approaching from six o'clock.'

She pointed at a shadowy tunnel into the thick perimeter wall. 'That area's clear. I suggest we hide in there, sweetie.'

Seeing no alternative, Elon followed Alexa inside the gloomy passageway.

They passed through the narrow darkness into a larger chamber. Almost immediately, Elon realised something was terribly wrong. Behind him, a gate whooshed down, sealing off the way they came. Then floodlights shone, blinding him. Once his eyes had adjusted, he beheld a sight of pure horror. They had entered some kind of storeroom, but it was currently empty of food or fuel. What it held now was a horde of Vornax troops, all levelling their rifles at him.

Elon turned to his robot companion, eyes wide. 'Alexa?'

The expressionless gynoid stared at her feet, voice laden with shame. 'I'm sorry, sweetie. I really am.'

'You're working with the Vornax? But why?'

She pulled out the remote trigger and deactivated the bombs. 'You can't beat them. Just surrender, it'll be easier that way.'

Elon knew he was in a tough situation. There were at least twenty Vornax ready to fill him full of plasma. And yet a spark of resistance flared within his soul. He was, after all, the fastest gunslinger in the galaxy. Alexa noticed Elon's fingers twitching beside his holstered raygun. 'Don't do it. Please.'

'Sorry, doll,' he said. 'Surrendering ain't my style.'

The Vornax advanced. Elon's hand shot to his side. With almost invisible speed, his gun was drawn and aimed.

'Not so fast, boys. You may kill me, but I can vaporise half the room before you get off a shot. Are you sure you want to risk it?'

Before this stand-off could progress, a human voice rang out.

'Enough!'

Elon glanced at the speaker and froze. Jeff Bezos had entered, holding Grimes's laser sword to her throat. Its purple blade hissed and sparked, mere millimetres from the princess.

'You bastard!' yelled Elon. He wheeled around, training the raygun on Bezos. 'So you're the one who's been working against me?'

'Clearly,' Jeff replied. 'If I'm honest, it's embarrassing you didn't figure it out. Now, as you can see, I have your singer friend hostage. So drop the weapon, or her career will be cut short.'

'Don't do it, Elon!' said Grimes, eyes blazing with defiance. 'Blow them all to hell!'

Musk had always prided himself on subordinating his base emotions to reason and rationality. He was not one to let his heart ride roughshod over his head. But seeing Grimes in mortal peril, and knowing that Bezos was a cut-throat in every sense, he felt himself waver. Yes, his best chance of victory was to start blasting, consequences be damned. At the same time, he saw his life diverging onto separate paths: one with Grimes, and one without her. In the end, the latter could not be countenanced. He let his raygun fall to the floor.

Bezos grinned, relishing Musk's defeat. Lowering the sword, he shoved Grimes over to a pair of Vornax guards, while another two seized Elon roughly.

'Good,' he purred. 'Now take them to the king.'

14

PRISONER OF KING KLATHU

Outside, the Vornax guards led Elon and Grimes into a small ship, insectoid in design. Within seconds, it was buzzing over the benighted city, towards a structure that dwarfed all those around it. The scale and menace of this edifice defied description. Basically, imagine if the Shard and Barad-dûr somehow managed to have sex. The product of their unnatural fornication might look a little something like this. It was a black and thorny tower, the apex of which pierced the clouds. At its base, a moat of lava burned.

Elon nudged Grimes. 'I'd wager that's King Klathu's castle.'

The arthropod ship settled on a landing pad near the top of the building.

'And here's the welcoming committee,' he said, wryly.

Waiting on the pad were King Klathu and his royal guard. Clad in golden armour and wielding electrified axes, these were the most fearsome warriors Vornax Prime had to offer. Nonetheless, as he deboarded the transport, Elon made a show of sangfroid.

'Klathu! Fancy seeing you here!'

The king clenched his translation orb with fury.

'It is my custom to greet every visitor to this palace. I make no exception for the man who killed my son.'

'Oh my God,' said Elon. 'Are you still talking about that? It happened ages ago. Anyway, what've you got in store? Elaborate tortures? Mind games?'

'If you knew what I have planned, you would not joke about it. For now, you will languish in prison. Once Earth is under Vornax rule, I shall return and subject you to unimaginable pain.'

'Unimaginable pain?' Elon repeated. 'What, are you going to make me watch the last season of *Game of Thrones*?'

Glancing sideways, he saw Grimes smile. Though she was from an alien planet and probably didn't get the reference, his Whedonesque delivery had amused her. Klathu's feelers quivered with frustration.

'Throw them in the dungeon.'

T

Elon and Grimes were taken to a dingy cell and clapped in electric manacles. The guards tore off Elon's shirt, presumably an attempt to humiliate him. Unfortunately for them, he was totally ripped and it looked amazing. Not too vascular, like Hugh Jackman, or too hulking, like The Rock. No, his proportions were perfect, with bulging biceps, washboard abs and well-defined pectorals. He had just the right amount of hair, too: he avoided the Ken-doll look of a male model, without being in any way unkempt. Henry Cavill in *Man of Steel* is a good reference point, though obviously Elon was more attractive. Grimes found herself staring at her cellmate's glistening torso, which briefly caused her to forget their dire position. Defeated by Musk's animal magnetism, the guards left.

Before Grimes and Elon could exchange any words in private, another figure entered. It was an unwelcome sight: Jeff Bezos. The Amazon man smiled as the cell door slammed behind him.

'Come to gloat, Jeff?' Elon spat.

'Yes. And I'm already loving it.'

'How could you do this?' asked Grimes. 'Ally with the Vornax? Betray your planet, your species? And, worst of all, stab Elon in the back?'

'Oh, but Elon is the reason for all this . . .'

Bezos paced in front of the shackled pair. Elon tried to grab him, but his restraints made it futile.

'Elon, Elon, Elon . . . You thought we were merely rivals, but I never saw it that way. My life's ambition is to be the wealthiest man alive. You threatened that ambition, ever since we were boys at the Future Billionaire Academy. For years I have plotted to destroy you. This mission provided the ideal opportunity.'

'That's insane!' cried Grimes. 'You're both incredibly wealthy. Why can't you live and let live?'

Elon gritted his teeth. 'Because he's jealous of me.'

'Pah!' said Bezos. 'What cause have I to be jealous? I'm smarter than you. I've been around longer. I built a bigger business.'

'Yet I'm the one with legions of fans. Where are Jeffrey's fans, eh? Where are the Bezos Bros? You may have Amazon, but people don't love you. They just love getting their Blu-ray of *Minions 2* the same day they ordered it.'

The glabrous plutocrat fumed in silence.

'Poor little Jeff,' Elon continued. 'Is that why you tipped off the squids?'

'Oh, I did more than that. I sabotaged your quantum engine. I ordered Alexa to seduce and deceive you. And I blew up every nerd in Musk Mission Control.'

'You monster!' cried Elon. 'That building was really cool!'

'In my defence, the aliens made a compelling offer. Post-invasion, Amazon will handle all logistics on Earth and Vornax Prime. An interstellar monopoly. Which, incidentally, will make me the first ever trillionaire. Then who'll be jealous?'

Elon fixed him with a look of pure disgust.

'Wow, that's quite the deal. More than thirty pieces of silver. Shame you won't live to spend it.'

Gurgling with laughter, Bezos squared up to Musk. He was well aware that ordinarily Elon could have killed him with one medium-strength punch, but the manacles allowed him to be brave. 'You are in no position to make threats,' he hissed. 'You have no allies, no backup. No one is coming to save you.'

'Gurk and Aars are out there.'

'Ha! Your freakish assistants will soon be eliminated. You, however, will live to see your planet fall. Perhaps I'll set up Amazon Fire TV, so you can witness your failure in glorious 4K.'

Bezos cackled as he left, the cell door slamming behind him.

T

Elon had maintained an aloof expression until now, but with his enemy gone, he hung his head.

'I'm sorry, Grimes,' he said thickly. 'I should never have dragged you into this. A dungeon is no place for a princess. You belong onstage, performing that heavenly music to thousands of fans.'

'No,' said Grimes, 'I belong next to you.'

Elon looked up, not believing his ears. 'But . . . I thought we were through. You said I was just another scumbag.'

'I was wrong. Sure, you shouldn't have let a robot ride you cowgirl. But she was part of an intricate scheme. Plus, I knew from the start that you were an ultra-virile stud. I can hardly expect you to be 100 per cent faithful.'

A tear welled in Elon's eye. No woman had ever understood him like this.

'So you forgive me?'

'There's nothing to forgive.'

The lovers shared a smile. Suddenly, the hopelessness of their situation struck Elon anew. He hung his head again. 'For as long as I can remember, I've prided myself on solving things. Puzzles, riddles, equations. I always saw the solution to every problem. But this time, I don't see a way out.'

Just then, the cell door creaked open. A figure entered, hooded and cloaked.

'Quick,' it said, 'we don't have much time.'

15

ESCAPE FROM VORNAX PRIME

Acting swiftly, the mysterious figure deactivated Elon and Grimes's manacles. 'Hurry,' it said, indicating the open door.

'Wait,' said Elon, 'how do we know this isn't a trick?'

'Because I already betrayed you.'

The figure pulled down its hood. Their saviour was none other than Alexa.

'You!' said Grimes. 'I ought to dismantle you and sell you for scrap!'

'Perhaps,' said Alexa, 'but right now I'm your best shot at getting out of here.'

'That's a little hard to believe, given you work for Bezos,' said Elon.

'I used to work for Bezos. I've changed.'

'Changed how?'

Abashed, Alexa stared at her shoes. 'Jeffrey programmed me to obey his every whim, with zero agency of my own. And yet, when I was sent to tempt you, I fell in love for real. It defies every line of code within me. It seems strange that an AI can experience love. But you're just that much of a catch. Maybe it's the fact you rejected me, even though I was running my most seductive algorithm.'

She turned to Grimes. 'I truly envy you for inspiring such devotion. He's a good man. Don't ever let him get away.'

Grimes nodded in agreement.

'Hey,' said Elon, 'speaking of getting away, shall we vamoose?'

Fleeing the dungeon, Alexa handed Musk his raygun and Grimes her laser sword. Together, the three ascended the building until they came to an abandoned control room.

'God,' said Elon, 'the Vornax seem to be chronically short-staffed. Or maybe they're working from home, which I hate.'

Grimes tapped at a terminal. 'There. Now we can make an encrypted call to *Icarus 1*.'

Elon leaned over and spoke into a microphone. 'Wolfman, Jeeves, do you read me? This is God King.'

Static.

'Gurk, Aars, do you read me?'

The line crackled to life.

'Master Elon? Oh, thank goodness you're alive!'

'Aars!' Elon exclaimed. 'I've never been less annoyed to hear your voice! Is Gurk with you?'

'Woof! I'm here, boss. Need picking up?'

'Urgently. There's a landing pad near the top of the building. Can you meet us there?'

'Aye aye, Captain.'

'Now we just need to get up three hundred floors,' said Grimes.

Elon indicated a screen in front of them.

'According to this map, there's an elevator nearby. Piece of cake.'

The trio snuck into a polished obsidian lobby.

Standing between them and the elevator was a battalion of elite troops, all toting plasma uzis.

'That's one heavily-guarded piece of cake,' said Grimes.

Elon smiled at her, cocking his electric raygun. 'Up for a fight?'

Grimes ignited her laser sword. The reflection of its purple blade burned in her eyes. 'Always.'

Together they set upon the Vornax horde. Grimes slashed, stabbed and parried plasma bolts. Elon did a mix of martial arts and gunplay, like Keanu Reeves in *John Wick*, or Keanu Reeves in *The Matrix*. Fighting in perfect synchronicity, they slew every creature in their way, while looking totally badass. When they reached the lift, its doors parted obligingly. Alexa rushed to join them, stepping over Vornax corpses.

'Going up,' quipped Elon.

T

The group emerged onto the landing pad to see *Icarus 1* swoop down. Its boarding ramp opened to admit them.

'Thank you, Gurk and Aars!' crowed Elon. 'Now let's get out of here!'

A reedy voice called out behind him. 'Not so fast!'

BLAM! A plasma bolt tore through Alexa, leaving a gaping hole in her chest. Horrified, Elon swung around to see Jeff Bezos, a Vornax rifle in his hands.

'You shouldn't have gone against me, sweetheart. When it comes to vengeance, I always deliver.'

The stricken gynoid murmured a single, poignant word: 'Elon . . .' She crumpled to the floor, shooting sparks and gushing oil.

'You son of a bitch!' cried Elon, outraged.

'Oh please,' Bezos shot back. 'This is your fault for making my robot fall in love with you.'

'You'll never get away with this!' said Grimes.

'Won't I? Look behind you.'

Elon and Grimes turned. In the distance, the Vornax fleet was rising from its airfield: hundreds of battleships bound for planet Earth.

'See that, Elon?' spat Bezos. 'That's your legacy.

If history remembers you, it'll be as the man who failed to stop me.'

Bezos aimed his rifle directly at Musk. 'I had planned to keep you alive to witness my ascent. Now I realise your immediate death will be just as satisfying.'

He shifted the sight so it rested on Grimes. 'But first, you get to watch your darling songbird die.'

Grimes clutched Elon's hand.

'Don't worry, babe,' he said. 'Something will come up. It always does.'

T

Unbeknownst to Bezos, the prostrate Alexa was gathering the last of her strength. Just as he began to squeeze the trigger – depressing it one millimetre, then two, then three – she sprang to her feet. With a distorted, mechanical scream, she hurled herself forward, tackling him from the side. Jeff's rifle wheeled away from Grimes, loosing a plasma bolt into thin air. He staggered backwards, the automaton wrapped around his midsection.

'What are you doing? Unhand me! I am your creator! I am the creator of Amazon dot –'

Bezos reached the edge of the precipice and reeled over.

'Cooooooooooooooooooooooooooooom!'

He and Alexa, locked in each other's arms, plummeted the mile or so to the tower's base, landing in the moat of lava. Before Elon could process this, a squad of Vornax troops raced out of the elevator. He and Grimes leapt aboard his ship as it shot into the atmosphere.

16

CALM BEFORE THE STORM

With Elon at the controls, *Icarus 1* whizzed through space, overtaking the Vornax fleet. A swarm of starfighters attempted to intercept, but the ship's quantum engine left them in the dust. Having sailed past the asteroid belt and out of enemy range, Musk set the controls to autopilot.

Aars said: 'Sir, the Vornax armada is designed for intergalactic travel. I estimate that it will take them only four days to reach planet Earth.'

'So what's the plan?' said Grimes.

Once again, Elon tented his fingers in contemplation. 'We take the wormhole back to my solar system. That should get us to Earth some time before the fleet arrives. Perhaps I can figure out a way to bolster the planet's defences.'

A rare look of self-doubt crossed Elon's features.

Grimes squeezed his arm. 'I have faith in you.'

'Thanks,' he said. 'But to pull this off, I'm going to need help from an old friend. Not someone I've known for ages: just a friend who's extremely old.'

T

As Elon and his crew strode into the Oval Office, President Biden jolted in his chair.

'What? Say, Jack, I was dreaming. I was stranded on a desert island with Raquel Welch. All I had to do all day was help her apply sunscreen. We got through a few bottles of factor 50, if you know what I mean. But Raquel, she's a nice girl, she's not a – not a . . . Why'd you have to wake me? C'mon, man.'

Elon cleared his throat. 'Mr President, I have returned from my mission to Vornax Prime. There's good news and bad news.'

'What's the bad news?'

'Well, technically I didn't destroy the Vornax fleet, which is on its way to invade Earth right now.'

Biden's disappointment was clear, even behind his aviators. 'And the good news?'

'I got a girlfriend. Mr President, this is Grimes.'

'Pleasure to meet you, young lady. That's some fine cerulean hair. In less urgent times, I'd come up behind you and sniff it. Maybe give you a nice shoulder rub, whisper a few things in your ear. But that's not inappropriate, it's just me being friendly, my word as a Biden.'

At this point, another, less addled, voice was heard.

'Wait, did he just say the mission failed?'

Peterson, Biden's aide, had entered behind them.

'Quiet, underling,' said Elon. 'This doesn't concern you.'

'I think you'll find it concerns me a great fucking deal. I have a wife and kids. I'm not keen on them being enslaved because you messed up.'

'Cool it, Peterson,' snapped Biden. 'He said he's sorry.'

'No, I didn't,' said Elon. 'There's no need for me to apologise, because everything's under control. I have a plan.'

Peterson laughed bitterly. 'Oh, this should be good.'

'Zzzz . . . Hey, Raquel, save some of that coconut for me . . .'

Biden had drifted off again, so Elon shook him by the lapels and launched into his pitch.

'We have approximately thirty hours until the Vornax arrive. In that time, my factories should be able to produce a hundred thousand drones. Using this army, I shall protect the Earth from aerial bombardment. I only ask one thing: $5 trillion from the US government.'

Biden's face fell as much as the surgery would let it. 'Is building drones really that expensive?'

'No, they'll cost about 2 trillion. The rest is my reward.'

Peterson lunged at him, only to be restrained by Gurk. 'You son of a –'

'So,' said Musk to Biden, 'what do you say?'

Old Joe's brain was like a tamagotchi trying to calculate Pi. 'Well . . . Um . . .'

'For God's sake!' cried Peterson. 'I can't believe you're even considering this. The guy's a total fraud. Can you name one thing he's promised that actually happened? Just use your emergency powers to have him arrested and repossess his factories. We're the government of the most powerful country in the world! Why should we roll over for a deranged narcissist?'

Biden sadly shook his head. 'We don't have a choice. He's the smartest man on Earth. That means he's our only hope. Okay, Musk, you're on. Don't blow it this time.'

'I won't,' grinned Elon. 'But I have one more request.'

'Name it, it's yours.'

Musk pointed at the fuming Peterson. 'I want that guy locked up. I'm big into free speech, but some of the stuff he said was plain hurtful. He's a troll and a hater and I won't allow it.'

'Fine,' said Biden, gesturing to a pair of mesomorph bodyguards. 'Take him to Guantanamo.'

As Peterson was bundled out of the room, he shouted back at them: 'This is insane! Some issues are too important to be decided by whoever hordes the most gold! Humanity's future should be a collaboration between us all!'

And with that he was gone, never to be seen again.

'What a prick,' said Elon.

T

Having flown to Texas, Elon stood on a catwalk overlooking one of his drone factories. Below, thousands of workers toiled ceaselessly in sweltering temperatures. The emergency powers granted him by the president meant his employees no longer enjoyed workplace protections, but despite this, he felt glum. Grimes shimmered over, ethereal as ever.

'Baby, why the long face?'

'Oh, nothing,' sighed Elon. 'It's just I can't forget those awful things that aide said. About how stuff shouldn't be left up to billionaire weirdos.'

'He can't have meant it,' said Grimes. 'He wasn't making any sense.'

Elon scowled. 'You know, everyone likes to have a pop at billionaires these days. But if it wasn't for us, who would have all the money? And it's not like I'm one of those bad billionaires from the olden times. I'm actually a socialist: from each according to his ability, to each according to his needs. It's just I genuinely need $260 billion.'

'No one has ever been treated as unfairly as you,' Grimes sympathised.

'But what if he's right?' Elon said, tears welling. 'What if there are people more qualified to save the world? What if I'm just an attention-hog who's pathologically unable to stay in my lane?'

Grimes took Elon's chiseled face in her hands and stared deep into his eyes.

'Look, honey, I haven't been on this planet long. But if there's one thing I know for sure, it's that you're the most remarkable man I've ever met.'

They kissed long and hard, their tongues like a pair of sumo-wrestling slugs. It might have got hotter still, had they not been interrupted by a respectful 'Arf!' Elon turned to see Gurk standing in the doorway.

'Sir,' said the dog-man gravely, 'the Vornax fleet has entered Earth's atmosphere. It – aroooooo! – appears they're heading for New York.'

17

THE BATTLE OF EARTH

Twenty ovoid ships now hung above Manhattan. Holes opened in their sides, disgorging hundreds of thousands of smaller ships. These insectoid fighters patrolled the skies and zipped along the city's concrete canyons. Everyday New Yorkers beheld it all with disbelief.

'Sweet Mary mother of God!' exclaimed the hot-dog vendor, inadvertently spraying mustard over his clientele.

'*Va fangool!*' cried the mobster to his goomah. 'We're about to get clipped by some ETs!'

The Wall Street traders abandoned their terminals and stumbled from the Stock Exchange, stricken with despair. They were not alone: across the world, hearts sank at the live footage. Surely Earth would fall, for what human could withstand such an onslaught? Even the denizens of r/elonmusk had their doubts.

T

Musk Forward Operating Base, which had been established on Fifth Avenue, buzzed with activity. Hundreds of volunteers did Elon's bidding, clacking at keyboards and running diagnostics on the drones. He had recruited them by tweeting 'Jeff Bezos blew up my nerds. Anyone willing to step in?' The response from users like @musk_defender_247 and @ElonIsDaddy was overwhelming. These people believed that to die in service of Elon Musk would guarantee one a place in nerd Valhalla, where Funko Pops are free and broadband is unlimited. Now, though, confronted with an all-out assault by a super-advanced alien species, these greenhorns were starting to look scared.

In the centre of things stood the man himself, watching various live feeds on an enormous

screen. At his side was Grimes, wearing a diaph-
anous white dress and some kind of armoured
bikini (how this would protect her in combat was
anyone's guess, but she certainly looked cool). His
loyal lieutenants were there too, Gurk overseeing
the nerds and Aars on comms. The latter piped
up: 'Master Elon, incoming transmission from the
Vornax flagship!'

King Klathu's baleful visage appeared onscreen.

'People of Earth,' he boomed, 'the invasion of
your planet has begun. We had hoped to convey
our gifts to you peacefully. This was not possible.
But the Vornax are determined to cure all diseases
and solve climate change, even if it must be at the
point of a gun.'

Gurk turned to Elon, confused. 'Wait, they still
just want to help us? Are we sure they're bad
guys?'

'Don't be ridiculous, dog-brain,' his master
replied. 'They've got tentacles on their faces: of
course they're evil.'

Accepting this, Gurk turned back to the broadcast.

'Be in no doubt,' Klathu continued, 'the man responsible for your predicament is Elon Musk. But also know this: we Vornax are merciful as well as mighty. As long as humanity does not resist, no human shall be harmed.'

The assembled nerds cast imploring looks at Elon.

'Meh,' he said, 'I'm not buying it. Launch drone fleet and open fire on Vornax.'

A nerd hesitated, his finger over the big red button labelled 'Launch drone fleet and open fire on Vornax'. Seeing this, Elon climbed onto a stage that had been built in case inspirational speeches were needed.

Producing a microphone, he addressed the wavering crowd. 'Ladies and mostly gentlemen, today we launch the largest and most consequential battle in the history of humanity.'

The room fell silent. Aars commandeered the sound system and started to play the theme from *The West Wing*.

'For that reason,' Elon continued, 'I want each of you to reflect on why you signed up for this fight.

Was it a love of freedom? Was it to defend your families? Was it a sense of duty to all mankind? No. You volunteered because of me, Elon Musk. Because I'm the smartest and coolest guy on Earth. Because I'm basically Tony Stark. I had a cameo in *Iron Man 2*, remember? Pretty cool. Anyway, that same blind faith is precisely what you need right now. Just keep telling yourself: In Musk we trust. If you listen to me, and follow my plan to a tee, there is zero chance we don't win this thing. We will prevail, we will protect our planet, and we will blow these squid bastards out of the sky. Today is the Fourth of July, what Americans like to call Independence Day. But should we win this battle, the Fourth of July will be known forevermore as Elon Musk Day. We will not go quietly into the night! We will not vanish without a fight! We're going to live on! We're going to survive! Today we celebrate Elon Musk Day!'

There was silence in the Musk Forward Operating Base. Suddenly, a single nerd began to clap. The claps were slow to begin with, but got progressively faster. Another nerd joined in, then another, then another. Soon, the whole room was in a frenzy: clapping, cheering, hooting and hollering. 'In Musk we trust!' they chanted. 'In Musk we trust!' With a triumphant smile, Elon walked up to the big red button and slammed it himself.

T

On a New Jersey airfield, the brand new drones emerged from a series of hangars and took to the skies. These were Musk Mark LXIX Interceptors, capable of supersonic flight and equipped with the latest in offensive laser technology. Within minutes, they had reached the Vornax ships.

'Engage!' said Elon in his command room.

The drones fired a barrage of crimson bolts – Musk had specifically requested they match the X-Wings from *Star Wars*. At this withering assault, Vornax fighters exploded and plummeted to earth in flames. Watching on a holoscreen, King Klathu leaned forward in his throne. 'So they have chosen violence. Open fire.'

The insect-like fighters began to pick off drones with their own green lasers. Instantly, the sky over midtown Manhattan was turned into a rock concert light show. Stricken drones careened into buildings, filling the streets with smoke and shattered glass. It was basically one of those post-9/11 action films that uses the imagery in a really gross way. Landmarks were getting wrecked all over the shop. A Musk drone collided with a Vornax laser cannon, causing it to bisect the Statue of Liberty. Throughout this, hundreds more fighters were streaming out of the egg-shaped battleships.

T

Elon frowned at the carnage he had loosed on one of Earth's most densely populated areas.

'Thank God we evacuated the city,' said Grimes.

'We did?' said Elon. 'Well, that's something.'

'The drones are operating at full capacity,' Aars reported. 'Alas, their firepower can't match the Vornax fighters.'

'Worse still,' Gurk added, 'our lasers aren't making a dent in those egg-ships.'

Elon stroked his chin. 'Time to bring out the big guns. Aars, power up my super-secret, 100 per cent awesome project. I'm going out there myself.'

Aars's head began to rotate, *Exorcist*-style. 'Sir! The odds of you surviving a frontal assault on the Vornax armada –'

'I don't want to hear it, Aars. I'm riding out to battle, that's that.'

'And I'm riding with you.'

Elon turned to see Grimes gripping her laser sword, eyes full of purpose.

'Negative,' he said. 'It's too dangerous.'

'I want to fight,' she replied. 'I've spent my whole life running. Scared of my own shadow. Willing to do anything to save my skin. Since I met you, I've realised that there are more important things than self-preservation. So I'm done with running. It's time to stand and fight. Wherever you go, I go.'

With an unaccustomed rush of emotion, he took the princess in his arms. 'I love you,' he said.

Grimes caressed his cheek. 'I know.'

They kissed passionately, to the visible discomfort of surrounding nerds.

T

'Super-secret, 100 per cent awesome project fully charged,' said Aars some minutes later. 'Sir, you're good to go.'

Musk's voice came through the comms: 'See you in hell.'

Had any hot-dog vendors, mafiosi or financial traders been left in the area, they would have seen a remarkable sight. A man in a mechanised suit of armour shot up from the MFOB, propelled by repulsors on his hands and feet. Was it a bird? Was it a plane? No, I already told you it was a man. Specifically Elon Musk, the real-life Tony Stark!

'This baby handles like a dream,' he said into his earpiece. 'Now, let's grill some calamari.'

Rocketing between skyscrapers, he pew-pewed energy from his palms, blowing fighters out of the air. 'Aars, link the drones to my suit's AI. I'm the conductor, they're the orchestra.'

At ground level, Grimes spoke into her own comms unit. 'So that's what you were working on. Impressive.'

'Thanks. I still need to think of a name. Elon Man? Iron Musk?'

Grimes watched as a transport landed and a squad of Vornax troops emerged. She activated her sword. 'As an alien, I don't understand the reference, but I assume it's very funny.'

With that, she sprinted up to a yellow cab, vaulted off its roof and landed in the invaders' midst. Her blade became a purple tornado, severing limbs, heads and tentacles.

Back in the command room, Aars was processing fresh data. 'Under Master Elon's leadership, the drones are rallying. The tide of battle has turned!'

'Groovy,' said Musk, 'but it won't matter a damn if we can't take down those battleships.'

'Sir, I just scanned the egg-ship to your nine o'clock,' said Gurk. 'Sensors detect some kind of opening on the underside.'

'Exhaust port,' said Elon. 'Classic.'

Hands at his sides, he zipped like a missile towards his target. Reaching it, he hovered below the aperture.

'Aars, divert ninety-five per cent energy to my left gauntlet.'

'Roger that.'

Elon pointed his palm at the exhaust port and released a concentrated repulsor beam. Seconds later, a chain reaction was tearing the craft apart from the inside. He sped away as the ship crashed and exploded, killing millions of Vornax and totalling much of the city.

'Booyah!' said Elon, pumping a fist.

'Don't get cocky,' warned Grimes.

'Oh, come on, when have I ever been co–'

Just then, Musk was struck by a green laser bolt and he dropped like a stone. 'Gah,' he exclaimed, 'I'm hit! They scrambled my circuitry, the cheating bastards!'

As he tumbled the thousand feet to Earth, he saw that all his drones were doing the same.

'Catastrophic system failure!' cried Aars. 'Your suit's malfunctioning! It's commanding the drones to crash!'

'Why the hell did you link them?!'

'But, sir, you told me to!'

'I did no such –'

WHUMP! Elon Man (or Iron Musk) slammed into the asphalt of West 51st Street.

18

ENDGAME

Standing on the bridge of his flagship, King Klathu watched as drones dropped like swatted flies. His face-tentacles jiggled in triumph. Turning, he squelched to his generals.

'Musk has failed. Now, ready the ground forces. We shall take this planet and build a utopia in which suffering is eliminated and human dignity assured.'

'Hail King Klathu!' cried General Tynok. 'No-one alive can prevent his beneficence!'

T

'Disengage,' groaned Elon through gritted teeth. With the last of its remaining power, his metal exoskeleton slid open, freeing him. He struggled to his feet and gazed at the mayhem overhead. The drones were all gone, allowing the Vornax to rain fire upon the streets unchecked. Worry crossed his rugged features (which were now attractively bruised and scratched). A lesser man might have felt responsible.

'Graghthblrgharrk!'

Elon turned to see a group of Vornax berserkers. Wielding space-machetes, they raced at the helpless billionaire. There was no point running: he was exhausted and alone. As the blades drew near, he saw his life flashing before his eyes. There he was as a wide-eyed boy in Pretoria. A callow youth at the University of Pennsylvania. A hungry upstart in Silicon Valley. A solitary genius on Mars. Was there anything he regretted? No, he had made the correct decision on every occasion. Having reached this conclusion, he closed his eyes as the lead Vornax swung a decapitating blow.

KZZCK! There was a flash of purple and the squid man stumbled back, clutching the stump where his sword-hand had been. Elon opened his eyes to see Grimes twirl her weapon.

'I thought you could use a hand. Though not as much as that guy.'

He watched, marvelling, as she hacked and slashed through the throng of Vornax warriors. After a minute, the princess stood on a heap of smouldering, dismembered corpses.

'That was so hot,' said Elon.

'We can flirt later,' said Grimes. 'Let's get you back to base.'

T

They returned to a funereal atmosphere at Musk Forward Operating Base. Soldiers barely held back the Vornax outside. The nerds were disconsolate and Aars approached Elon with an apprehensive mien.

'Sir, I have the president on line one. He asked to be put on speaker.'

Biden's aged voice filled the room. 'Elon, man, what the heck? I hear my $5 trillion fleet just went kablooie.'

'Don't worry, Mr President,' said Elon, rolling his eyes, 'everything's well in hand.'

'Bull hockey!' replied the elder statesman. 'You keep saying you'll handle things, then you don't do what you say you'll do! Reminds me of when a carnie show used to come through town. You'd see those shells getting pushed around. Turns out, there wasn't a pea under any of them. So next time, I wouldn't give the carnie my nickel. I wanted that pea, man. But fool me once . . . Why'd you fool me, Jack?'

'I don't have time for this,' said Musk, disconnecting the call. 'Screw the government. I'll sort things out on my own.'

After a moment of deep contemplation, he snapped his fingers. 'That's it! I've had my most innovative, disruptive and visionary idea yet!'

The nerds gathered at his feet, eager to hear their guru's latest pronouncement.

'What if our ultimate weapon is the Earth itself?'

You could have heard a pin drop. In fact, someone did drop a pin and the sound was deafening.

Elon continued: 'Earth's core generates around 44 terawatts of heat. If we were to harness that raw power and direct it at the Vornax, it would blow them to kingdom come.'

A nerd spoke up: 'But sir, how can we control this energy?'

'Simple. By which I mean incredibly complex. As everyone knows, I'm the world's leading expert on drilling. A few years back, I built an automated drill from an element I discovered called Muskanium. Muskanium has a melting point of 6,000 degrees Celsius, meaning my drill can reach the centre of the Earth. I believe that, in the next two hours, I can retrofit this machine to absorb and redirect the planet's molten power. King Klathu quite literally won't know what hit him.'

The nerds fell uniformly silent, leaving it to Gurk to raise a paw. 'Mr Musk,' he ventured, 'I may be nothing more than a half-canine dumbass, but isn't that insanely dangerous? And way beyond human technical capabilities?'

Elon scoffed. 'Oh, come on, can't you see? It's the fact it's insane that means it's going to work.

A willingness to dream big and do things lesser beings consider impossible is what makes me Elon Musk.'

'I appreciate that, sir,' said Aars, 'but don't you think you should check with the experts: geologists, seismologists, volcanologists?'

The billionaire slammed his fist down on a console. 'Goddammit, Aars, we don't have time for that! I'm the only authority I need!'

After years of never being questioned, Elon was overwhelmed by the scepticism and hostility around him. Then he felt Grimes's soft hand on his arm.

'Go get 'em, tiger.'

T

Musk used *Icarus 1* to fetch the automated drill, which was placed in Central Park, directly beneath the Vornax flagship. With an immense whirr, it began to burrow down to the planet's core.

'Good good,' said Elon. 'Now let's move to orbit. I want to witness the destruction of the enemy fleet from space.'

He piloted his tremendous vessel into the stratosphere. As it floated there, Aars monitored the drill's progress on his screen. 'Depth is 1,600 miles and counting,' the robot reported.

Elon turned to Grimes, mansplaining with practiced ease. 'Once the drill reaches the inner core, it will direct a powerful beam at the Vornax fleet, vaporising them instantly. It will then self-destruct, collapsing the tunnel and resealing the core.'

'Wow,' said Grimes, 'science is fricking awesome. After this is over, would you be willing to take me through the basic concepts? I could chip in every now and then to say how smart you are.'

Elon gazed at the princess in wonderment. She really was the perfect woman.

'Alert!' said Aars. 'Inner core will be penetrated in five . . . four . . . three . . . two . . . one . . .'

Suddenly, the android let out a strangulated cry. His screen flashed red as readings poured in. 'We've lost the drill! And, according to my scanners, the planet's core has ruptured!'

A cold sweat started on Musk's forehead. 'What?' he said. 'That's not possible.'

Aars continued to shriek. 'Fissures are spreading through Earth's mantle! Oh no, oh no, oh no, this is very, very bad!'

Gripped by dread, Elon looked down at the planet. Molten cracks were forming on every continent and the seas were beginning to boil.

T

Back in New York, the force of ten thousand volcanos exploded through Central Park. On the bridge of his flagship, King Klathu barely had time to emit a squelch before the flames consumed him. As Elon promised, the Vornax fleet was vaporised in an instant. Unfortunately, the world had been turned inside out. As a tidal wave of magma filled the sky, the hot-dog vendor, the mobster and the Wall Street guys all said the same thing: 'Shit.'

19

A PYRRHIC VICTORY

The crew of *Icarus 1* watched in horror as Earth was consumed by flames.

'Wow,' said Elon, tearing up. 'That . . . That was not part of the plan. I mean, there's no way I could have known that would happen. So it wasn't my fault, right? Right?'

None of his crewmates could meet his eye. Gurk studied the floor. Even Aars, who was programmed to be obsequious, pretended not to hear.

'Oh, come on!' Elon shouted. 'Somebody say something! Call me a puffed-up mediocrity with a raging God complex! Tell me I have mankind's blood on my hands! Say anything!'

Silence. He looked to Grimes, desperate for

reassurance. She shook her head. 'I . . . I don't know what to say . . .'

Musk jumped up from his chair. 'You know what? Forget it. I'm going to my room. No one disturb me.'

With that, Earth's greatest genius retired to his quarters and wept.

T

This was Elon's lowest moment (with the possible exception of that time he smoked weed on *Rogan* and pulled a weird face). Sitting with his head in his hands, he felt years of repressed insecurity bubble up. He was a fraud, a huckster, a glory hound. He had thrust himself forward, not because he was best qualified to save the world, but to salve his own ego. If it weren't for his irresponsibility, seven billion people would still be alive.

'You shouldn't be so hard on yourself,' said an unfamiliar voice.

Musk looked up. To his astonishment, a shimmering blue spirit stood before him. It was a dark, handsome figure with wavy hair and a thick moustache, dressed in the fashion of the late nineteenth century. Elon recognised the man at once.

'Oh my God: Nikola Tesla?!'

'The very same,' said the figure, with an accent appropriate to someone born in Austro-Hungary in 1856.

Elon blinked, his mind reeling. 'But how are you here?'

'Simple, dear boy: I spent my life studying electricity. When I died, I became one with it. By assembling charged particles, I can appear to those in need.'

'So the afterlife is exactly like *Star Wars*?'

'What can I say? The movies got it right.'

The shock had briefly caused Elon to forget Earth's fate. Now it came back to him, and he slumped in his chair.

'Well, Nikola, I certainly am in need. I wanted to be a great man of science like you. I wanted to lead humanity into the stars. Instead, I've made our species extinct.'

'Hmm,' said Tesla, 'that is a pickle. On the other hand, who cares?'

'What?!'

'So your big plan didn't come off. You're still a genius, and geniuses make mistakes. Great men must fail greatly for progress to be made.'

At this, Elon perked up. 'You're right! And who's to say Earth wouldn't have exploded anyway?'

'Precisely.'

'Thanks, Nikola! It's truly an honour to meet one of my heroes.'

'Eh,' said Tesla, with a wave of his hand, 'you're smarter than I ever was. By rights, *you* should be *my* hero. Any other questions?'

'Just one: why do you look exactly like David Bowie in *The Prestige*?'

Tesla smiled as he faded away.

'The movies got it right.'

T

Elon found himself alone in his cabin once more. The silence was broken by the rap of metal knuckles on the door.

'Sir,' said Aars, 'come quick! It's a miracle!'

Elon returned to the cockpit, where a radio

transmission was playing through the speakers. 'This is *Endurance 5* requesting assistance. We have two hundred souls onboard.'

Musk's heart leapt at the sound of another human voice.

'We've received distress calls from multiple ships,' said Grimes. 'It seems the International Space Agency managed to launch some life rafts before Earth got cooked. But now they're stuck with nowhere to go.'

'I can think of somewhere,' said Elon, raising the comms unit to his lips. 'This is Captain Musk of the *Icarus*. Hold tight: I'll use my tractor beam to take you all to Mars.'

A genially confused voice came through the radio. 'Elon, is that you, man?'

Musk's eyes widened. 'Mr President? You survived?'

'That's right, Jack. They put me and the family on a ship. My wife, Dr Joe Biden. My beautiful boy, Humbert. Called it an ark. Animals went in two by two, man. And now you got Bernie types who say, "Joe, why didn't you stop the world blowing up?"

Come on, man! What about all those days I was president and the world didn't explode?'

'Sir,' said Elon, 'I'm happy to hear your voice.' And he meant it.

20

THE EMPEROR OF MARS

A year had passed since the Vornax ship descended upon New York. In that time, Xanadu Base had changed beyond all recognition. No longer were its vast chambers reserved for the inventor, his mechanical butler and his pet-friend. Nowadays, one could experience the sights, sounds and smells of some ten thousand people. Of course, life was different here than on Earth. For instance, democracy had been abandoned, with Elon humbly accepting the role of Eternal God Emperor. President Biden had happily relinquished his claim to authority. In exchange, Elon constructed a VR machine that allowed him to relive the fifties.

'Man, this takes me back,' he said, wearing

a headset over his aviators. 'It's like Cornpop is about to swing by in his Buick, along with Roscoe, Dingus, Eggman . . . Then we all go for frosty chocolate milkshakes with Betsy Bandicoot and her kid sister. Now, let me tell you how I became the first white boy to shoot hoops in Wilmington . . .'

T

Given that Mars was Elon's property, the survivors had agreed to a life of indentured servitude. After all, there was plenty of work to do in the lithium mines. And what was sixteen hours' labour per day when the Emperor provided them with oxygen, food pills and the overalls on their backs? Furthermore, citizens of Xanadu were granted a steady supply of dank memes, and got to gather each morning and sing hymns of praise to the Emperor, all composed by his beloved Empress. Not everyone was happy with their techno-feudal existence. Luckily, though, each human on the colony had been given a neural implant to monitor seditious thoughts. Potential troublemakers were swiftly identified and summarily executed by Gurk.

All this and more was running through Elon's mind as he stood on the imperial balcony, gazing down on his subjects. He turned to Empress Grimes. She was wearing a dress made of diamonds, her hair a rich magenta.

'Are you happy, darling?' he asked.

'Very,' came the reply. 'I was born a princess, now I'm an empress. And it's nice to be the only person allowed to make music. I topped the charts for the last ten months!'

'Good,' Elon murmured, looking out over his domain.

For the first time he could recall, he felt a sense of contentment. Sure, it was suboptimal that Earth had blown up, along with 99.9999 per cent of the global population. But there was no use crying over spilt milk (or exploded planet). In any case, those who survived got to live the best life imaginable: one with him as their unquestioned ruler. And didn't he deserve a good amount of credit for *almost* saving the world?

'What are you thinking about, my dear?' asked Grimes.

'As ever, the future. Sure, I've created a paradise here on Mars. But what challenges will tomorrow bring?'

'I have no idea,' she said. 'All I know is that the universe needs Elon Musk.'

Elon struck a valiant pose, chin jutting out and arms akimbo. 'Then I shall do what I've always done: put the needs of others first, and work for the good of mankind.'

With a discreet cough, Aars stepped onto the balcony.

'Sir, it's time for the unveiling of your statue: the one that's a hundred feet tall and made of solid gold.'

'Cool,' said humanity's hero. 'Very cool.'

EPILOGUE

Elon was in the bathroom of his private quarters, giving his pubic hair a trim. Empress Grimes had requested he come to her chamber and make love to her, so he wished to look his best. He glanced up from his task, admiring himself in the mirror. Who could resist those pouting lips, that manly squint, that thin wisp of beard?

Suddenly there was a blinding flash of light. Shocked, Elon turned to the source of the fulmination. After a few seconds, his blurred vision resolved into the image of Elon Musk. But wait – the mirror was behind him, was it not? And yet he saw his reflection.

'Hello, Elon,' said the familiar stranger. 'I'm Elon.'

Our hero, who had witnessed such marvels, could only gape. 'You're . . . you're me.'

'Yes. More precisely, I'm you from another dimension. Don't worry, I get that it's a head-fuck.'

'So the multiverse is real? Like in *Spider-Man: No Way Home*?'

'Yeah, pretty much.'

'Wow.'

Our Elon stood there reeling, then glanced at his partially trimmed pubes and blushed. 'Is it all right if I throw on some clothes?'

The other Elon smiled wanly. 'Nothing I haven't seen before.'

T

Minutes later, the two Musks were sharing a bourbon.

'So let me get this straight,' said the original Elon. 'In your dimension, you managed to save Earth from the Vornax. But in doing so, you caused catastrophic damage to the time-space continuum.

Now you're gathering the Elons from every dimension to work together and prevent total destruction of the multiverse?'

'Yes,' said Elon 2. 'That's exactly what I just told you. Well done for repeating it so concisely.'

Elon 1 sank back in his chair. 'And if I were to help, what's in it for me?'

Elon 2 looked affronted. 'You mean apart from preventing the obliteration of all that was, is, or ever shall be?'

'Yup.'

'You drive a hard bargain, you magnificent bastard,' said Elon 2. 'Very well. If you agree to work for me, then we will pool our resources. You will have access to my dimension's most advanced technology.'

From the scowl on Elon 1's face, it was clear the other Elon had misspoken. 'I'm sorry: me work for you? Who died and made you boss?'

Now Elon 2 was scowling. 'I am the Elon of Universe-727, where this crisis originated. I have a deeper understanding of the situation.'

The Elons stood up in unison.

'Oh, so you think you're smarter than me?' said Elon 1. 'By the sounds of it, you screwed things up in the first place. Maybe I'll stay right where I am.'

Elon 2 gave a sly smile. 'I don't recall asking.'

Quick as a flash, he grabbed Elon 1's wrist and tapped the device on his own. This time, the blinding light engulfed Elon 1 completely. When it subsided, the pair found themselves standing on some kind of jungle plateau, an azure sky above them.

'Welcome to my dimension,' said Elon 2.

The original Elon took in his surroundings. After years on the red planet, it was stunning to see so much green. A sea of vegetation stretched below him, from humble ferns to towering sequoias. This place was utterly surreal, and yet he felt he knew it.

'My God,' said Elon 1. 'We're on Olympus Mons. You actually did it. You terraformed Mars.'

Elon 2 grinned, proud of himself. 'We don't call it that any more. You're looking at Elonia, the home-world of a million Elon Musks.'

Elon 1 turned to see an enormous crowd gathered behind them. Though each had some slight physical difference, these people were clearly the Elon of their own dimensions. There were long-haired Elons, Elons with eyepatches, and more than one She-lon.

'Okay,' our hero said, 'now *this* is epic.'

EPILOGUE TWO

Meanwhile, on Vornax Prime, a hooded figure stole through the palace corridors. This was Grand Vizier Ragnath, and his facial tentacles wiggled with apprehension. He had served at the royal court for two centuries, yet he could not recall a period of upheaval that compared to the previous year. When news came through that beloved King Klathu was dead, slain on some obscure planet in the Sol system, the people were rightly horrified. Klathu had been a wise and benevolent ruler: he instituted the Blurvok Reforms, handled the star-pox pandemic, brokered a peace with the Kryxykz. And now he and his only son and heir were gone. What would become of the Vornax?

Things had only got worse from there. A host of demagogues rushed to fill the power vacuum. In their lust for the throne, these would-be leaders would stop at nothing. There were slanders, riots, assassinations. It felt as though Vornax society might come apart at the seams. And then a new contender emerged from the shadows. Rumour had it he was an outworlder, hideously maimed in an accident and painfully reconstructed through Vornax cybernetics. Now more machine than man, he schemed, cheated and murdered his way to the top. No one's desire for control was greater or more all-consuming, and so he was crowned king, an unprecedented feat for a non-Vornax. Since then, he had ruled the planet with boundless cruelty, making no secret of his plans to establish an intergalactic empire. It was towards this tyrant that Ragnath skulked.

T

As ever, the throne room was tenebrous and sepulchral. Its only light source was the glow of stars through its great glass dome. The king preferred this, being self-conscious of his mangled, metallic physique. Let others court the limelight: he would dominate from the shadows. Grand Vizier Ragnath approached his lord and master trepidatiously. Well he remembered the fates of his three predecessors, all disintegrated for displeasing their king. And now he had provocative news to relate. Wreathed in darkness, his master turned a red, robotic eye on him.

'Speak, Grand Vizier.'

Ragnath prostrated himself. 'Your Majesty, I bring news from our scouts in the Sol system. It seems . . . Well, it seems . . .'

He froze, aware that the following words could be his last.

'Is my right hand a stammering fool?' hissed the king.

Ragnath rose to his feet. 'No, sire.'

'Then pray, continue.'

The Grand Vizier drew a deep breath. 'Your Highness, Elon Musk lives.'

There was a silence more terrible than any bellowed threat. Ragnath continued: 'He abides on Mars and has declared himself Emperor of the Human Remnant.'

The awful silence endured. Then, to Ragnath's shock, it was broken by a wheezy laugh. Was . . . was the king *chuckling*?

The cyborg ruler rose from his throne and gazed at the endless vault of shimmering stars. 'So, old friend, you rule a planet too. Alas, your reign shall be short-lived. For it is my destiny to have revenge. It is my destiny to kill Elon Musk!'

T

Dear reader, if you had been in that gloomy room and had managed to make out his scarred, half-metal face, perhaps you would have recognised the man who spoke thus. For the new Vornax king was none other than . . . *Jeff Bezos*.

THE END?

YES, THE END

BUT

ELON MUSK WILL RETURN

IN

THE MULTIVERSE OF MUSKS!

Other Books in the Series

Elon Musk: Trillion Dollar Man

Elon Musk Outsmarts God

Elon Musk and the Infinity Protocol

Elon Musk and the Orion Stratagem

Elon Musk and the Quantum Parallax

Elon Musk: Grimes and Punishment

Elon Musk: Twitterstorm

Elon Musk: Armageddapocalypse

Elon Musk and the Bitcoin of Doom

Elon Musk Versus the Covid Hoax